NOW YOU DON'T SEE ME

ALEC PECHE

GBSW PUBLISHING

ACKNOWLEDGMENTS

I would like to thank my first reader, GM, for the inspiration for this story. I had wanted to try writing a paranormal thriller, but more of a story about a single person with special talent, rather than an entire cast of paranormal characters. We discussed which talent my protagonist would have and she suggested teleportation.

What could a superhero woman do to save the world with such a skill? There are endless possibilities!

I'd also like to thank my editor Ellen Falk for being such a teacher of grammar and sentence structure. Now if I can just retain her teachings for the next book.

Alec Peche

ONE

Michelle Watson, CIA Case Officer, reviewed her final checklist before embarking on her mission. Food, weapons, heat sources, keys, smartphone, maps, lock picks in a backpack. Check. She nodded to her superior, Officer Meeks. Sheila Meeks nodded back. Michelle took a deep breath, closed her eyes, and briefly imagined Captain Travis Cox's prison cell inside the Siberian prison. Milliseconds later, Meeks looked at the empty air as Michelle had disappeared into the vapor.

They timed her arrival to the middle of the night in the far eastern Siberian time zone. She suddenly appeared inside the cell that contained the American captain who was kept in solitary confinement. He appeared to be asleep in his bed. Michelle hoped he was asleep rather than in too poor a shape to escape. She had briefly visited a week before to learn the layout and to update the captain on an escape plan. Prison conditions were tough, and she hoped he hadn't assumed that she was a mirage when she appeared.

She nudged him awake. His initial response was one of defense against attack. Then he realized who was there.

"Wake up and dress warmly. We're going to get out of here," she whispered. She also handed him a high-calorie nutrition gel to give him energy. "Here's a battery-operated warm vest to put on. It will help keep your core warm. Grab any coats you see along the way."

He dressed and swallowed the nutrition gel quickly, then nodded.

"Ready."

"Okay, I have lock picks and C4 to get us out of here. I'm going to try to pick the lock outside first. The moment the door is open, move to your right and follow me," she said, handing him a gun with a silencer attached to the end of the nozzle.

Then, as the last time, she disappeared before his eyes. He'd never seen anything like that before. If she hadn't visited once before and left him a bunch of nutritious gels to build up his energy, he would doubt his sanity. She was no mirage; she was his superhero.

Michelle appeared in the corridor just as a guard entered the cell block. When she saw him, she moved instantly behind the guard and watched him as he surveyed the corridor staring at where she first appeared. She followed behind him as he walked, checking the cell doors to be sure they were locked. In this section, prisoners were not behind bars. They were behind solid metal doors. When he reached the cell where Captain Cox was located, she pulled a small canister out of another pocket and dropped him like a fly by blowing an anesthetic gas at his face. She removed the keys from his belt and soon had Captain Cox's door open. She removed a gun from the guard's holster and quickly took the guard's jacket off, giving it to the captain.

It was fortuitous that she had the guard's keys as it would take less time to open the three doors standing between them and the Siberian wilderness. The CIA had hacked into the prison's security cameras and played them feed from a different time rather than the actual feed so Michelle and Cox wouldn't be caught on camera. She disarmed one other guard on their way out, and soon they exited the prison and walked in the cold deserted street of the town. They estimated they would have twenty minutes before an alarm was sounded. They needed to hustle quickly to a snowmobile parked on the next street. Michelle had laid out the escape plan as Cox dressed. He knew he had to survive a thirty-minute ride to a pick-up location. He had noted that Michelle could leave him at a moment's notice, if necessary, to protect her own safety. As long as she was conscious, she could escape. They pulled out snowmobile suits from a storage bin located at the back of the snowmobile and put on the very cold clothing. In under a minute, they roared out of the town on a single snowmobile in their thermal suits with helmets hiding their faces.

Snowmobiles were a common form of transportation in Siberia, so they weren't making an unusual sound. However, they were unusual in the middle of the night. Still, it was the best way to escape. Their helmets had night-vision goggles, so they could drive the snowy landscape without lights.

They were meeting a quiet electric-powered small aircraft that would take Captain Cox toward the Russian coast and across the Bering Strait into Alaska. Michelle would drive the snowmobile back and get home by her usual travel method. They just needed the aircraft to take off before the Russians noticed it. She knew the town didn't have a helicopter or small plane at their disposal, so they would search by truck or snowmobile.

So far, so good. The side mirrors of the snowmobile showed no lights following them or even visible. The rendezvous spot was picked based on the ability of a plane to land on skis. There didn't need to be a paved runway, just a relatively flat space. The designated landing place had a hill between it and the prison town. Hopefully enough to hide the snowmobile lights, which she would turn on to aid the plane's landing. Once the pilot had control of the plane on the ground, they would turn off the snow-mobile's lights and switch to a single flashlight. They practiced the maneuver in Alaska before she visited the captain the first time.

Michelle and the captain were able to communicate through their helmets, and he watched the plane's approach on a smart-phone she'd given him.

"Travis, when you return to friends, family, and co-workers, make no mention of my special abilities. Tell them a Seal team rescued you and you can't say more than that. Nobody would believe your story, and you have no proof. Likely your friends will think you went crazy in prison or you were hit on the head. Are we clear?"

"Yes, Ma'am."

"Good. Have a safe journey home."

"Thank you, Michelle, for getting me out of that hellhole. I can't wait to return to American soil."

The plane was three minutes out, and they had a little farther to go, but her heart rate picked up when she could hear alarm bells ringing in the town. In the stark, cold landscape, the sound traveled far. Still, there were no lights behind them. She hoped there weren't visible snowmobile tracks. The plan was for the plane to fly away from the town while it climbed in altitude so it couldn't be hit by gunfire on the ground. Some bullets reached ten thousand feet, and it would take the small light plane some time to climb.

The CIA was monitoring the town, and so far, no one was heading their way. According to the app, the plane was in the final approach, so Michelle shut the snowmobile's engine off and turned on its headlight. She couldn't see the plane, but she could hear it. They saw a large black shadow touch down, and as soon as the pilot was safely breaking, Michelle turned off the headlight and instead turned on a flashlight. She felt Captain Cox get off the snowmobile behind her to approach the plane. When he reached the door of the plane, she turned off her flashlight.

The pilot texted her that he was ready to depart, and she moved the snowmobile and its headlamp to light up the snowy landscape for the plane's departure. The moment the wheels were up, she shut the light off and began the journey back toward town. Ideally, she would like to park the snowmobile in town so their contact could return it from wherever they had acquired it. She would travel to Alaska and wait for the plane to arrive. That way, she would be close if they needed more assistance. Fortunately, her special talent was not related to the distance she needed to travel. No matter the actual distance, she could be there in a flash. After she first discovered her travel abilities, she used a stopwatch to see how long it took her to travel five-thousand miles away versus going outside to her back yard, and the time it took was the same.

The plane should land in under an hour in Wales, Alaska. If it ran into trouble, it could land sooner on Little Diomede Island, located in the Bering Sea, but the hope was to make it to Wales on the Alaskan coast. Once there, the captain would transfer to a bigger plane to head for a military base in Fairbanks.

Michelle was about to reach the edge of the slope that was the path down to the city. The alarm bells were louder here. She pushed up the night vision shield of her helmet and pulled out a set of binoculars to get a sense of the commotion below. What she saw alarmed her. She would have to make her escape without returning the snowmobile.

A few snowmobiles and a military truck were fanning out around the city, including heading up the slope that she was occupying. She thought for a few seconds about what to do. She decided she would start the snowmobile and head down the slope aiming for the military truck and tie the throttle to the handlebar, and she would disappear before impact with the truck. That would distract the searchers and potentially stop them from looking up to the sky and spotting the plane. A Russian military plane could quickly shoot it down. If the crash was fiery enough, they might assume the escaped prisoner died in the crash.

She carried out her plan and reappeared behind the truck on the edge of the city. A quick look around revealed that no one had noticed her appearance, and she watched the explosion between the snowmobile and the truck. It wasn't huge, but the searchers wasted a lot of time talking and looking through the wreckage for their escaped prisoner.

Michelle glanced down at her phone app and saw the plane was approaching the Russian coast. Perfect. They might just make it out of here alive and well. After the little plane was over the Bering Sea, no longer over Russian land and nearing Little Diomede Island, Michelle put her phone in her pocket. Once the plane flew past the island, it was in American airspace. She would head for Wales and wait for the plane. Then, she was heading for a warm destination as the Siberian cold was awful.

Little Diomede Island was home to a group of Alaskan natives. In the early morning, the silence was deafening. She watched the plane pass over the island and marveled at how quiet it was. If she didn't have the app on her phone, she wouldn't have believed there was a plane above her in the sky. Another sixteen miles, and it would reach mainland Alaska. She hopped over to Wales and saw the plane was on approach to the airport, and she could see a bigger plane parked and ready to take the captain on to Fairbanks.

The moment the little plane landed, Michelle was off to meet with Officer Meeks for a debriefing, and then it was on to some place warm. Given that Officer Meeks was in Virginia, she might just shed the snowmobile suit and head for the Caribbean. She looked at her watch, doing a calculation of the time in Virginia.

She had crossed so many time zones in the past three hours or so that she had to pause to calculate what day and time it was.

She reappeared in front of Sheila Meeks, who jumped at her appearance even though she had sent her a text warning her of her imminent arrival.

"Sorry, I can never get used to your ability to appear and disappear to wherever you set your mind to."

Michelle smiled and was tempted to tell her superior that she was just as surprised by her special talent. Given the heat of the office, she began to unzip the snowmobile suit as she described the operation. Sheila likely knew all the information Michelle told her from their spies and satellites, but it was good to confirm and to hear if there was any news out of the prison town about the escape.

"Captain Cox's plane is in the air to Fairbanks, so we can consider him a successful mission."

"What do the Russians think happened?"

Sheila smiled and said, "They seem to be at a loss to explain what happened. They don't understand why they can't find a body in the wreckage between the truck and snowmobile."

"Good. Keep the Russians guessing."

"That was a brilliant idea on your part. With your special talent, you could stay on the snowmobile much longer than an ordinary driver and aim it perfectly."

"I was also hoping to distract the Russians. I didn't want them to notice the light plane in the sky above. While it was out of range of bullets, I don't know enough about rockets or other military weapons to know if they could be found in the dark. Better to keep them focused on the ground."

"Again, a brilliant idea. I'm sure the Russians will figure out the US had a role in the captain's escape, but I'm glad they can't figure out how we got it done."

"Okay, well, I'm off to some place warm. Siberia is unbelievably cold, and kudos to the Alaskan natives that live on Little Diomede Island. I could never live somewhere so remote, barren, and cold."

"Unfortunately, I have another mission for you. The good news is it is not a frozen and barren landscape like Siberia. The bad news is you have little downtime. We're having a briefing tomorrow morning at seven. As it is approaching two in the afternoon, you only have a few hours to pop into some place warm."

"Darn. I was so looking forward to some time off. What's the mission, and why do you need my specific skills?"

"I'm as in the dark as you are. An order came to me from high up in the command, so we'll both get briefed tomorrow."

Michelle did a calculation in her head of where she wanted to go for about the next eight hours. She decided she would head home. Not to her Virginia condominium, but her home in San Martin, California. It was warm there, and she always enjoyed visiting her family. Moments later, she disappeared from Sheila Meeks' office.

TWO

When Michelle discovered her special talent while in her mid-forties, no one had been more surprised than she. Everyone who lived in San Martin had special talents of some sort. Mostly they could breathe magic into their occupation to make it something special. The town was a tourist attraction as all the shops have that little something in their products. From bakeries to florists, photographers to the organic farmers' market, the products were the best. Outsiders didn't know the secret of the town. They just appreciated what they found when they visited.

Michelle had grown up with no special talent that anyone could discover. She left to go to college, joined the police force of another city, married, divorced, and raised two children. One day while she was on the job, she was having a pity party as she felt pulled in two directions. She loved the town and the people she'd grown up with, but she was unhappy that she had no special talent. She did a routine traffic stop with her mind elsewhere, and it took a trauma center to bring her back to life. Soon after she was released from the hospital, she discovered her paranormal ability. She could travel anywhere she put her mind to. By the time she'd made a full recovery from the gunshot wound, she knew what did and didn't work in her travels.

The next question was what to do with her special talent. It wasn't like she could open a magic bakery with her travel skill. Even if she held someone's hand, she couldn't travel with them. She could teleport herself and the clothes she wore and whatever she had loaded in the clothing's pockets or the backpack on her back. Anything held in her hands didn't travel with her, be it a friend, a luggage handle, or just a cup of coffee.

How could she put the teleport to good use? No one else in her paranormal city had her ability, nor did anyone have an explanation of why it took so long for her talent to reveal itself. She spoke with friends in her hometown to see what they suggested she do with the odd skill. Months of discussion led her to approach the CIA. Surely, there was a use for her talent as a spy? She could make a getaway from a scene that perhaps no one else in the world could do.

Once she made up her mind where to use her new skills, approaching the CIA and demonstrating those skills took some planning on her part. It was such an impossible skill that she had to make sure her teleport skill was believable. After proving her talents to various leaders, she was assigned to a special secret division with few people aware of what she could do. America had a secret weapon in her, and they needed to keep her identity and skill away from the rest of the world. Michelle wanted to keep her talent hidden as she would be the personal target of any enemy country.

When she joined the CIA, Michelle Watson's one rule was they couldn't send her on a mission to kill someone. She wanted nothing to do with killing someone in cold-blooded murder. It would be too tempting for the CIA to have her appear next to some awful dictator and kill them before disappearing. They had tried ordering her on a few such assignments. Not only had she turned them down, but she also tendered her resignation from the agency. They refused her resignation, signaled their understanding of her line in the sand, and no longer tested her resolve. Furthermore, any weapon that she traveled with had to travel with her in a clothing pocket or backpack, eliminating many guns that were too big to fit.

So far, she had spied on other governments and rescued Americans like Captain Cox. She wondered what the next assignment was going to be. She guessed she would find out in the morning.

In the blink of an eye, she made an appearance in a barn on her small farm in San Martin. She had designated the barn as it was a safe place to reappear. She wasn't likely to be run over by a car or tractor or scare someone popping into her kitchen. While her close friends knew of her special ability, no one else did, including her adult children. When she first discovered the talent, she tried to tell her older child, but she assumed that Michelle was hallucinating after her injuries. She decided never again to try and explain. Her kids had their own lives, but she still managed to see them regularly. They always wanted to visit her home, as they wanted to stop at the wonderful bakery. Little did they know they were eating magic baked goods. After she nearly died from the gunshot wound, she'd told them that she would work for the FBI as a data analyst and was therefore safe from other violent criminals. They wanted to believe her explanation, and so she kept a condominium in Virginia but frequently visited the small farm in California.

Michelle walked out of her barn and sat down on a chaise lounge on her back patio for a nap in the sun. She had checked her children's plans for the day, and in the narrow window that she would be in California, she would not be able to meet with them. She set the alarm to wake her in an hour and settled in to enjoy the late winter temperature in the low 70s. She was startled awake an hour later by an obnoxious bird's chirping, a full three minutes before the alarm was to sound. Still, she was happy with her warm nap. As she had seen no one, she decided to head back to her Virginia condo, given the early start she had in the morning. It was dinnertime in Virginia, but still mid-afternoon in California. Time zone hopping was the most disorienting side effect of her transporting skill.

Soon she settled into her Virginia condo with plans for dinner, a glass of wine, and a good book. She would get up early to work out at the gym at the agency's headquarters. She needed muscle and endurance for her assignments because while she could move fast by teleporting herself away from danger, she often needed a mix of combat and teleporting skills to save her life or that of whomever she was rescuing. Sometimes the milliseconds it took her to teleport herself were enough of a lead for a criminal to do damage to her. Quick reflexes could, on occasion, save her as well as disappearing from the scene.

THREE

Michelle completed her workout and showered before presenting herself to the conference room at the appointed time. In the room were several people she'd recognized from prior assignments. There was also a new man she hadn't met before, but he looked to be around her age. She put him over six feet tall. He had a look of both relaxation and yet eyes that missed nothing. She'd learned early in her time with the agency that agents eschewed polite introductions and handshakes. Knowing someone's name, real or fake, was on a need-to-know basis. Then Tina MacDonald walked in, and she immediately knew this was going to be a difficult assignment.

MacDonald was the spy agency's second in command. She had personally observed Michelle's special talent, and then she had not seen her again for four or five years. There was also the unknown man.

"Thank you, everyone, for coming in today. Michelle, I understand after your recent Siberian jail rescue, you hoped to have some vacation time in a warm climate. Alas, we need your skills paired with Mr. Smith."

Ah, Michelle thought, Mr. Smith was the mysterious man she hadn't been introduced to. He was a spy, and Michelle wondered if his real name was Smith. Probably not. It was just a cover.

"We have an unverified rumor of a problem brewing here at home with worldwide implications. We just hear whispers in corners of the world, and we don't know what the full picture is or, frankly, even if it is true. However, we're worried enough to expend resources to find out if there is a glimmer of truth."

Michelle wondered what the case could be about. She hadn't had such a vague assignment before. She waited for more detail. Fortunately, Mr. Smith was equally uninformed and said, "MacDonald, I think you'll have to give me more explanation than that. I have no idea what this mission is about."

"We think we may have an industrialist from the US so worried about the effects of global warming that he may try and eliminate every source of oil worldwide."

"How?" asked Officer Meeks with a frown.

"How would you do that?" MacDonald asked, playing Devil's Advocate.

"I guess I would destroy every oil refinery and any major oil fields in the world, then move on to the pipelines that transport them. You could bring the world to its knees the moment you limited both the production and refining," offered Smith.

"That's a good start. How would you destroy these oil fields?"

"Somehow, I have to think that if I sent an army of one-hundred explosives specialists with C4 to blow up these sites, I would be stopped before I could do enough damage. What does our industrialist have in mind?"

"Understand that there are hundreds of major oil fields worldwide on land and sea from the United States to Russia and many countries in between. If our industrialist was to target all these locations, they would have to hire hundreds of explosives experts. So, what's the other approach?" MacDonald asked the group.

The silence stretched for a minute, and then MacDonald continued.

"How about if you target the six largest oil-producing countries–Venezuela, Saudi Arabia, Canada, Iran, Iraq, and Russia? These six countries account for about seventy percent of the world's oil."

"Okay, so you need twelve explosives specials, two for each country, assuming the reserves are close in location. However, I think we're talking large swaths of land, more than C4 could effectively disrupt. How about if you sent planes and dropped bombs from the sky to blow things up? Six planes and crews with lots of bombs," Michelle suggested, but her tone indicated she knew next to nothing about dropping bombs from the sky.

"You're getting closer, Michelle, but it's actually a far more awful plan. Our intelligence suggests he's going to drop nuclear bombs on the oil fields."

"Oh my God," was nearly everyone's response, along with a few expletives.

"Wait, where can you get a nuclear bomb? It's not like there's even a corner of the dark web that sells that item," Smith said.

"Our intel says he's mining uranium and has figured out the use of a centrifuge to enrich it. It comes out of the ground as U-238 and is less than one percent pure. After it is enriched by centrifuging with many acids, it reaches about ninety percent to be weapons-grade plutonium-239."

"That sounds easy to do. Why isn't everyone making nuclear bombs?" Michelle asked. "Sorry, but I'm not a geology or chemistry wiz."

"It takes large centrifuges that spin at something like sixty-thousand rotations per minute. Your average blood spinning centrifuge in a medical laboratory rotates at less than a tenth of that speed-wise. You are also dealing with a substance that requires protection from radioactivity. So, this takes extraordinary equipment, time, and effort to achieve. Some experts in the US think that Iran, with its forty-five hundred centrifuges, can make enough weapons-grade plutonium in a year. Imagine what might happen if a smart American industrialist put his mind and his fortune at work on the subject."

Everyone nodded, understanding the timeline and resources it would take, and each could think of a billionaire that might be able to pull it off.

"So how do we confirm this intel, and what do we do to stop it? I don't understand physics, but dropping a bomb on a room filled with centrifuges spinning uranium sounds explosive, no pun intended," Smith said.

"That's where you two come in. I'd like you to be able to confirm our intel," MacDonald said.

"You're both experts in your skill areas. Smith has the ability to fit in anywhere. He is the master of disguise. I want him to get close to our suspect. Michelle can travel without being seen. We need her to explore various locations to see if there are centrifuges at work."

"So are we working together as partners, or are we off on completely separate tasks?" asked Smith.

"Officer Meeks will be directing you two and reporting directly to me with all updates from you. She is more accessible than I, and it's important that we don't lose time conveying any new information. If our intel is wrong, we need to quietly bury this investigation. If it's correct, we'll need to take action. Like all of our missions, you are sworn to secrecy. Not only do we not want our industrialist to be aware of our investigation, but we also don't want to give the rest of the terrorist world an idea of how to cause great harm. Is that clear?" MacDonald said, looking at the two agents individually for acknowledgment of their under-standing.

MacDonald got up and left the room. Michelle was left with the mysterious Smith, Meeks, and three intelligence experts who she knew were about to brief her with more details.

One of the agents started a slide show with information about the case. He showed pictures of uranium in its natural state, and then there were pictures of what happened during the processing to enrich it. Thirty minutes later, Michelle felt she could identify the components she would see in an enrichment center. Next, there were slides from satellite images of where uranium deposits were found on earth. The CIA's computers tracked who owned the various uranium mines and where it was sold. Finally, they listened to an extensive biography about David Niemi, their industrialist--his net worth, houses, companies, family, and life experience.

At the end of the briefing, Michelle concluded that he had the money and the brains to fund such a concept. He had to be mentally ill to think it was okay to try and stop global warming by killing off large swaths of the planet's population. People would die from either dropped bombs or eventually by hunger as crops were no longer harvested and sent to market without oil for farm equipment or transportation.

"What's the timeline on this? Does he need a year to enrich uranium or a week?" Michelle asked. "Has he acquired enough uranium yet? Do we know where the centrifuges might be?"

Smith added, "Does he have a team of scientists? Who did we get the intel from? Any suggestions on where I should insert myself into his life?"

"We don't have answers to your questions, Officer Smith. All we know is Mr. Niemi has the capacity to do this. Officer Watson, we have no answers to your questions other than to say the uranium enrichment process takes about a year."

"So at this point, this truly is just at the gossip stage, and you're looking for some additional data first and foremost to verify any possibility he might be working on enrichment. MacDonald has started this operation based on the fear that Mr. Niemi may have the resources to do this," Smith summarized. "It's up to Watson, Meeks, and me to come up with a plan."

"Yes, that sums up the situation nicely," Meeks said. She then looked over at the analysts and said, "Thank you for the briefing. We'll work on a plan and don't need your help at this point."

There was silence in the room as the analysts left. Finally, there was just Michelle and Jason Smith seated with their supervisor, Officer Meeks.

"Well, Meeks, any suggestions on how to proceed?"

"Yes, here's my plan," she said and proceeded to lay out what she wanted the two agents to do.

They nodded, and Smith asked, "I like everything in the plan, but I don't see how Michelle is going to travel to all of the locations on your list in such a short time. Did the agency buy a used Concorde jet?"

"Actually, Michelle is perfectly capable of visiting these locations in the timeline. As MacDonald said, she's a wiz at travel. Are you ready to move out on your assignments?"

Smith and Watson nodded, and the conference room emptied.

Smith stopped Michelle outside the room and said, "I need your contact information so we can keep up to date on findings."

They exchanged contact information, and then Smith added, "There's some secret about you that no one seems to want to tell me. I guess I'll know in time."

Michelle smiled enigmatically and replied, "Yes, I'm special, and I'll see you in the field when you least expect it."

Michelle headed for a stairwell, and once the door closed behind her and she was sure she was out of the sightline of everyone, she teleported herself to her Virginia home and set out to plan her teleporting activities. The list they gave her of potential centrifuge sites was large. Worldwide she had some four hundred locations to visit. She needed to group them by location, time zone, and camouflage clothing she would need to fit into each location. In some locations, she would wear all-black clothing, and in others, military camo, and areas that were frozen like the Siberian location, all-white clothing was the way to stay hidden against the snow.

With some places, she was sure she could pop in for less than five minutes, while other locations might require that she spend a few hours exploring. She also needed to Google Earth each site so she could be sure she didn't pop into a busy street and get herself killed by a car before she could disappear. She spent the remainder of the day looking up each location, taking a picture, and in some cases locating a place close by where she could appear and neither raise suspicion nor accidentally die.

By the next day, she began planning her site visits, methodically going through the list, starting with properties Mr. Niemi was known to own. She rather liked this assignment as it would test her transporter skills. She'd never tried to go to, say, twenty different locations in a day. She had no idea if that would make her tired. She hadn't noticed in the past that transporting made her tired, but there was always a first time for everything.

FOUR

Before she set off on her search, she sent Meeks and copied Smith on the locations that she planned to visit that day. Meeks acknowledged her plan but provided no comments while Smith asked "how" she planned to be in so many places at once. She decided to act like she hadn't seen his email and instead went to work moving around the earth with just a few tools. Her pockets contained a cell phone and pepper spray, and she had a knife on one ankle and a small revolver on the other. She would use her cell phone to take pictures, and the other items were for defense. She also wore body armor and a helmet to protect her if she should land in the middle of a dicey situation. She also had identification, some protein bars, and a bottle of water.

Her first location was a private island in the middle of Indonesia. Uranium enrichment like cool more than heat, so she planned to visit the hot locations first and eliminate them as potentially manufacturing nuclear weapons.

She thought uninhabited islands were the easiest to scout and knock off the potential centrifuge locations list. Toward dawn, she had pictures from each location and zero evidence of any centrifuges. She sent her pictures to Meeks and Smith and went to bed in her Virginia condo. She had weeks of this reconnaissance of locations ahead of her. Given a twelve-hour day, Michelle could knock off up to twenty locations a night.

The second day of work in Southeast Asia provided no evidence of uranium enrichment. When she arrived home, she sent her photos out to her team. She was just coming out of the shower, and she heard her doorbell ring.

Michelle was alarmed as she wasn't sure she had ever heard the doorbell ring before. Who would be ringing in at 7:30 in the morning? It was too early for salespeople to bother, and she'd never been visited by a neighbor. Besides, she was in her bathrobe, and that left her vulnerable. Stopping to grab her gun and view the front door camera, she was surprised to see Smith standing on her doorstep.

She supposed she could leave her condo, but she had nothing to fear from the man. She opened the door and, after a moment, invited him inside.

"Jason, what are you doing here at this hour of the day? Was our mission canceled?"

"Not that I know of. No, I dropped by as my life may depend on you in the future, but there's something secretive about you that Meeks and you know but aren't telling me."

"I'm sure it's just your imagination. I'm just your average covert agent. We all have that attribute of secretiveness about us."

"Yeah, right. You must own some top-secret superfast plane and helicopter. You've moved around the earth with speed beyond normal commercial or military planes. You even visited places without runways."

"Maybe I'm just copying pictures off the Internet and pretending that I'm visiting these locations."

"That was the first thing I checked. The pictures you sent

Meeks and me are original. You've been to these places. How have you done it?"

Michelle hated to lie to her first "partner," but her skill was top-secret. She would rather be considered weird than let her secret out. If they needed to at a future time, she would tell him about her skill. There was a chance that he would never need to know about her transportation abilities. She knew for her own safety, she had to keep them hidden from the world.

She decided to just change the subject. "What have you discovered so far?"

"The agency is still building my cover. I'll be a wind power generator company CEO. The agency is adding pieces about me in the appropriate journals and databases. I have another week of doing nothing more than figuring out what you're up to. Then I assume the identity of James Stout, CEO of Wind Century, and I'll begin to make inroads into Mr. Niemi's life."

"You could visit some of these locations in the interim," Michelle suggested.

"No way could I begin to duplicate your productivity on this one. Even if I was already in Indonesia, I still couldn't have visited the number of locations you did. Besides, I'm studying about being an executive in the wind power field."

"Then why are you bothering me this morning? I need to get some sleep."

"I want to understand how you're moving so fast around these locations," Jason asked. "Are you using an unmanned plane? Do you have a network of unmanned planes at your disposal?"

"Perhaps I have ownership of a network of satellites, and I just have to connect to them and start snapping pictures."

"Perhaps. I'll have to research that."

"Okay, well, if that is all, . . ." Michelle said, indicating she was ready to close the door.

"If you're snapping satellite photos, why are you only doing that at night? Wouldn't that be better during the day?"

"Do your research, and you'll figure it out."

He stood up to leave, tossing over his shoulder, "If we're ever to serve as backup during a critical incident that could lead to one or both of us dying, you better have told me the secret."

"Yes, sir," Michelle said, giving Jason a military salute before closing the door.

She had a smile on her face and settled down to read in bed, knowing it would help her nod off to sleep. Time would tell if he needed to learn about her special skill, but she liked the fact that he was thinking about how she could take the pictures she had. On that thought, she settled in to sleep.

FIVE

Two weeks later, Michelle had worked through about half the locations with no evidence of any centrifuges. Her partner, Officer Smith, had checked in with Michelle one more time to try and reason how she'd been able to gather the pictures. Then he went undercover, and she heard nothing more from him other than reports relayed through Meeks.

The research department that had collected the images noted that she might chance upon people. She took care to dress, similar to the locals adding theatrical makeup to change her features to assimilate.

First on her list today was a closed copper mine in Colorado. Normally, these locations were deserted, but recent images showed some human activity.

While she had a special skill to transport herself anywhere, an underground place like a mine could be tricky unless she had the tunnels memorized. She was vulnerable to falling, bumping her head, or suffering some other calamity inside the cave.

She studied images of the cave's entrance and imaged herself standing outside of it, and milliseconds later, she was standing where she imagined. She quickly looked around to see if anyone spotted her and saw someone getting something of a trailer attached to a pick-up truck. The man seemed to be blinking as if wondering if Michelle was real.

She looked around for a place to move to and soon found herself underneath the pickup truck lying on the dry dirt. She heard the man mumble, "What the heck?" which made her smile. Then she heard him add, "I must be going crazy seeing a woman out here," and Michelle grinned.

Then she settled into doing her job. She took pictures of the area and waited for the man to move whatever product he had in the trailer into the cave. She heard him call someone on a walkie-talkie and ask, "Did you see a woman walk into the mine?"

She silently laughed when she heard a response of, "Is the sun too hot, or have you been drinking on the job, Ray?"

"No, I must have been seeing a mirage as there is no car here either, and I don't know how you would get here without one. But, don't mind me, I'll be in with a load shortly."

She wondered where the second man was located. He couldn't be too far away as most technologies didn't work inside caves. She heard the sounds of a dolly moving down the ramp and wondered what was on it. Soon she saw Ray pushing a dolly toward the mine entrance with a large cardboard box on it. What was in the box? As she watched the box head for the mine entrance, she gathered video. Later, the resources at the CIA could read the writing on the box and perhaps determine what was in it. For now, she would follow behind Ray and his dolly to see what they were up to.

She appeared at the entrance to the underground area and listened for noise to see if anyone was close by. Hearing nothing but the sound of the dolly bouncing over an uneven surface in the distance, she slowly made her way inside. It was instantly warmer by at least ten degrees. Caves were heated and cooled by the earth's surface rather than cold or hot air found at the entrance to the cave. Today she enjoyed the warmness of the earth's crust rather than the cooler ambient air temperature of a Colorado spring morning. She looked back at the truck and decided that there could only be these two men and one vehicle. She didn't have any way to see in the dark other than using a flashlight that would alert the men to her presence. She decided instead to go explore the trailer. She thought she would hear the dolly's noisy movement, and if she was wrong, she would have to transport herself out of the trailer.

She walked up the ramp into the trailer and looked at the assortment of boxes. Many were the same size. She listened for another minute but didn't hear the wheels of the dolly. She went over to the largest boxes, of which there were many of the same size in the trailer. She looked for a way to open the lid and decided she would undo the tape and then restack the boxes to hide where she pulled up the packaging tape.

She opened the box and was puzzled by what she found. It didn't look like any of the centrifuge pictures she studied. However, it was some kind of lab equipment. She took a bunch of pictures and quickly restocked the boxes before disappearing from inside the trailer as she heard the approaching dolly noise. She had the foresight to look around this time before she exited the trailer and teleported herself behind a small tree. From the tree, she watched two men approach the trailer. They were talking, but Michelle was too far away to hear what they were saying. Though she loved her special teleporting power, she thought about an old TV show, *The Bionic Woman*, and wished she had the listening skill that the character had in her bionic ear.

As she watched, the man who had momentarily seen her before she moved under the truck gave a look around at where he had seen her standing and then shook his head, which made Michelle smile. The two men each had a dolly loaded up and were soon wheeling it into the mine. As she knew there were additional boxes they needed to remove from the trailer, she timed the amount of time it took them to return and noted it. That would give her a distance to go look when she visited this mine later. Once they loaded their dollies again and headed inside the mine, she went back inside the trailer to take photos of some smaller boxes. She debated what to do next—move on to her next location or wait for these characters to leave so she would know when she could explore the defunct mine and access what they were making inside. It was early in the day, so she decided to work on the next location.

The next several locations on her list were mines. The CIA computer had sorted through a list of abandoned mines of nearly a half million in the United States alone. It had greatly narrowed the list to just thirty locations that Michelle needed to visit. The other mines were either too small, caved-in, or otherwise inaccessible. She spent the remainder of the day visiting dark and creepy mines and finding no evidence of anything other than bats in them.

It was time to head back to the first mine and hope the two men were gone for the day. She teleported to the tree she'd hidden behind earlier in the day. The truck and trailer were gone. She used a pair of night-vision goggles and looked around for other shapes but saw nothing. She then switched to a thermal image goggle, and other than a deer family in the distance, there was no living creature in the area. Michelle entered the cave making slow progress turning the light on and alternating with the thermal goggles. She really had no other way to see her way through the extremely dark space. She was relieved to come to a room containing the cardboard boxes, and she saw that no one was in the area keeping a watch on the equipment. She took photos, then followed the cave a little farther, but nothing was happening. She carefully made her way outside and was dismayed to hear a noise outside. She teleported herself to the tree then looked around to see what was making the noise.

It was the same truck and trailer from earlier. She debated waiting around to see if this shipment was the same as before. The same two men exited the truck and walked to the back of the trailer. They opened the doors and began loading the dollies. Michelle waited until both men went inside the cave to do a quick search of the trailer. The boxes looked identical, so she took a few pictures and then teleported herself home.

"Oh my gosh!" Michelle exclaimed, a hand over her heart.

The person sitting on her home's sofa was doing the exact same thing. It was hard to say who scared whom more.

"How did you get inside my home?" Michelle asked.

"I picked your locks."

"I'll have to get new door security."

"What the heck did you just do?" asked CIA Case Officer Jason Smith.

"What do you mean?" replied Michelle with all the evasion she could muster in her voice.

"One moment, I was the only person in this room, and in the next blink of my eyes, you appeared. How did you get here?"

"How long have you been in my home?"

"Three hours. How did you get in here? You didn't come through the front door."

"You were asleep when I walked in, so you missed my entrance."

"No, I wasn't. I've been practicing my undercover role as the wind energy company CEO and just sat down. Seconds before you arrived, I was standing where you're standing. If I hadn't moved, you would have bumped into me."

When Michelle first explored her teleporting skill, she had

knocked over a few people when she suddenly appeared nearly on top of them. She had since learned to verify in advance where she was planning to appear to make sure someone wasn't standing in her way. She had one more ace up her sleeve to try on Smith.

She moved behind him in the room and then spoke, "See, you're just not observant. You didn't turn around when I moved behind you."

The point she made momentarily made him doubt his powers of observation. He stayed alive as a CIA operative through his skills at deception and his powers of observation. His partner, in this case, had special movement skills, and he was determined to understand how she was able to move about the world. He'd watched her appear in her living room out of thin air, and now he was fairly sure she'd just moved around her home in the same manner. He didn't believe in magic but could think of no other reason to explain her ability to move around the planet.

"Actually, Watson, for the first time in my nearly fifty years of existence, I may believe in magic. Somehow, you seem to be moving around the earth faster than a human could do. You're my partner, and I've been on some extremely dangerous assignments in the past. I want to know that I can count on you. It's either that or I will have to ask for reassignment, and that will put this investigation back for several weeks while they find someone new to work with you. I looked your record up, and you've never worked with another partner since you joined the CIA. Now I think I know why. Meeks knows of whatever special talent you have, and that's why she gave you the assignment she did. So, what's it to be? Are you going to come clean and tell me how you move around so quickly, or am I going to ask to be assigned to a new case?"

Michelle had known that this moment would come. This was indeed the first time she'd been assigned a partner, and Smith was correct in saying the way any operative stayed alive was to be highly observant. She could waste their time and set back the agency's timeline to understand the threat posed by David Niemi, or she could come clean.

She sighed and sat down, gesturing to Smith to do the same.

"I do have a special talent, and you're correct I haven't worked with a partner before."

"So tell me about this talent."

"I was shot in the line of duty during a routine traffic stop, and it nearly killed me. A trauma center saved my life. After I was discharged from the hospital, I discovered that I had a new talent besides having a few new screws and stitches in my body. I can teleport myself anywhere in the world. Though I admit, I haven't thought of trying to land on the International Space Station. Once I discovered the skill, I had to figure out where to put the ability to the best use. I did a little research and then approached the CIA. I believe there are two, and now you make three, people who know of my ability. It's why I haven't had a partner up to this point. I'm a national security secret; if word gets out about my talent, there would likely be a huge bounty for my capture and killing."

"Wow. That's a gift and a burden. Kudos to you for doing something good with the skill. Can you take me with you if we hold hands or something?"

"No. I can't even take a suitcase. When I teleport, I can only take the clothing on my body, a backpack, and whatever is in my pockets. Nothing more."

"Too bad. We could bounce around the world solving problems for the CIA."

"I can, and I am doing that for the CIA."

"Touché."

"I hope you have no intention of telling anyone—a co-worker, your wife, your shrink of my special skill. It would be career-ending and perhaps life ending if word gets out."

"You're my co-worker. I have no wife or shrink, though if I told your story to anyone, they would probably line me up with a shrink. I'm usually pretty cynical about the world, but Michelle Watson, you're the real deal. You're a good person, and I'm honored to work with you."

Michelle released the breath she had been holding as she'd waited for his response.

She looked into his eyes, trying to guess if this was a line of poppycock or if he truly meant it. She thought he was sincere, but he had to be a good actor with all the undercover work that he did.

"If you try to move with a gun in your hand, does it go with you?"

"No. It has to be in my pockets or backpack. I have managed to tuck a rifle into a long side pants pocket, but anything in my hand gets left behind."

"Weird."

"I know the teleportation thing is strange."

"No, I think the pocket/backpack thing is weird. The rest is pretty cool. I'm glad you decided to use your talent for good, and I think you picked about the best agency in the US to serve and to protect you."

"Thank you. I'm good at escapes, so I don't think I need much in the way of protection, but thank you for thinking of me personally."

"So if I grab your wrist or cover you with a blanket, you can still teleport? How about dreams? Have you ever moved somewhere in the middle of the night because you were dreaming?"

"Two things prevent me from moving—sleep or unconsciousness. I've tried entering a bank vault long after the bank closed, and I got in and out."

"One final question, and we'll move on to our case. Can you do a demo of your teleporting ability by moving around your living room?"

Michelle proceeded to move from one side of the room to the other with no footsteps in between. *What a useful skill in a fight!* Smith thought as she ended her demonstration and headed for her kitchen to get them both a drink.

SIX

The next morning Meeks had scheduled an in-person meeting. Michelle was at least halfway through the list of potential centrifuge sites, and the location she spent so much time at the previous day deserved more exploration though no one thought the supplies that were moved were indicative of a future centrifuge site.

Meeks noticed the temperature had warmed up between her two agents. Then, with a little probing, she validated her thought that Michelle had shared her special talent with Case Officer Smith.

"Let's get started. Michelle, you're making good progress scoping the locations. Jason, you're about to go undercover and insert yourself into Mr. Niemi's world. We're going to lose contact with you other than cryptic text messages. We've done everything possible to make sure your cover is airtight, and we're spending a lot of money providing you with the trappings of an executive interested in green energy."

"Yeah, I've been thinking about that, and I think we have to change a few things."

"Like what?"

"I think I need a few toys powered by wind. I'll stick with the private jet, but I'll need a battery-powered car, an off-the-grid-powered home somewhere, and a solar-powered boat that I'll park in San Diego as our friend has a boat parked in that yacht club."

"We can do the car, but the home and the boat on short notice? I don't think so."

"It's easier than you think. Here's a broker for solar boats, and they lease them. Here's another listing for large wind-powered homes. As a wind farm executive, I would, of course, power my home with wind, right?" Smith said, passing some pages to Meeks.

"This is expensive."

"Yes, but as a wind farm executive, I would have these toys, right?"

"Hell, I don't know. I've never met one."

"Well, I did my research, and our Mr. Niemi has toys beyond your imagination. I'm not a billionaire CEO, so I don't have to have those toys, but I do need a few to belong and show the strength of my devotion to green energies. I need to demonstrate the whole zero-carbon footprint thing. In fact, I'll pass on the agency's private jet and fly commercial as I can sell that as generating fewer carbon emissions."

"That's quite generous of you to pass on the private jet," said Meeks sarcastically.

"Actually, you should be grateful, as it is by far the most expensive thing on the list of toys," said Smith with a smirk.

"Boss, if it helps, I don't need anything on my side of the house," Michelle said, joining the fray.

"As if," Smith said. "With your talent, you're saving the agency all kinds of money they can spend on me. So really, as a team, we're likely the most cost-effective team ever at the CIA."

"You're making my head hurt with all of your cheerfulness, Smith. Why don't you go back to being the grim undercover agent."

"It's your fault for pairing me with Michelle. I'm excited about this assignment. I think we have one of the best ops I have ever been on at the CIA. Michelle is doing excellent work scouting the locations, and now I must be as good in my role as the Wind Century CEO. I need some tools to do that. I would hate if I studied all that wind technology stuff for nothing. That's wasted brain space that I'll never get back."

"Okay, I'm not happy with these last-minute changes, but I do agree with your thinking on the topic. We'll have the car, boat, and house for you by the time you arrive in San Diego. How are you going to meet Mr. Niemi?"

"Through the yacht club where my boat will be parked. When our target is in town, he goes out on his boat daily, even if it's only for an hour. The dude likes to sail. So I'll make sure I cross paths with him at the dock or the club."

"Oh gosh, don't tell me you want us to buy a club membership," Meeks looked in alarm, thinking about the expense.

"No, they have visitors from time to time, and I'll just be one of those."

"Do you need any help?" Michelle asked.

"You could pop in for dinner at the club on occasion," Smith said. "I'll think of a cover for you."

Sheila Meeks compared the advantages and disadvantages in her head for her two agents to be together.

"Michelle, as long as you aren't seen by someone in Niemi's orbit as you continue to visit these sites, you two can be seen together. Perhaps your presence will provide more cover for Jason."

"Jason, call me when you need me and message me what the appropriate attire is, and I should be able to accommodate most of your engagements. Sheila, did the staff figure out what those pictures of equipment in the cave mean?"

"Yeah, they think it's going to a be a meth lab of large proportion. It's a good place for that as manufacturers often have explosions which are how they're discovered. It looks from a map that no one would notice if there was a cave explosion. It's really deserted. We'll probably want you to go back in a week or so to see what progress they've made. What we can say is that there are no nuclear centrifuges in any boxes."

"I'll add that location back on my schedule. From the little conversation I overheard, the two men unloading the equipment were not nuclear scientists!"

They discussed the operation a little. The research department at the CIA had been unable to find an uptick in nuclear centrifuges such as those made for nuclear power plants. Mr. Niemi, the industrialist, could purchase the metals needed to make his own centrifuge and bury those purchases inside one of his companies.

So far, the rumors of this wild idea of blowing up all oil resources seemed far-fetched. The three CIA officers hoped it stayed that way.

SEVEN

Michelle resumed her globe-trotting, including visiting the cave site thought to be a future methamphetamine manufacturing site. She popped in every few days to monitor the assembly of a meth lab, and then she checked about a week later and found her entrance to the meth lab blocked by rubble. Her guess was the lab blew up. She smiled at the thought of an illegal operation blowing up as soon as it had been set up, but then she worried that there might be survivors on the other side of the cave collapse, so she put a call into handlers at the CIA to get someone to take a look at the location. She had no idea when it collapsed, and they might already be too late, but that was for someone else to worry about.

She checked her watch and decided she was done for the day. She was tired from the constant travel. She used focused imagery to make sure she landed in the exact right place. Fortunately, if she thought of a sandy beach with waves, she didn't teleport there as there was nothing to specifically identify it. Wherever she traveled, she had to use unique frames of reference to get there. A generic sandy beach image sent her nowhere. She was glad she learned that in the early days of exploring her skill. Otherwise, she would be panic-stricken that she would be endlessly traveling around the world.

Her phone vibrated, and she saw a text from Jason:

Hey, you want to drop into SD for dinner at the yacht club? Dress is anything casual and sexy.

She thought about how tired she was and what she had planned for the next day. Still, she decided it was important for them to be accommodating partners. Her appearance might help him advance his role as the CEO of Wind Century.

She texted back, *Just finished my day, need to pop home for shower and change of clothes, be there in an hour.*

They traded another text on where she should meet him. It was a little early for dining, but she'd already had a long day and wanted to be home before midnight East Coast time while dining in a time zone three hours away. Moments later, she was inside her townhouse and frowning as she looked through her closet for something that met Jason's specifications.

Michelle was slender and put significant time into lifting weights. Finally, she settled on a sundress that showed off her firm shoulders and arms and a sweater in case it was cool near the water. She put her auburn hair into a messy bun, selected a small necklace and dangling earrings, and grabbed chunky heels in case there were wooden boards that could grab a narrow heel. Her dress had pockets, so she placed a small purse in one pocket and her cell in another, and she was ready to teleport to San Diego.

She suddenly appeared on the deck of Jason's rental boat parked in the harbor. It had been dark in Virginia when she left, and she found herself squinting into the bright sun and was momentarily blinded.

"That was an on-time arrival."

"Yeah, well, going from nighttime to bright San Diego sun is painful," Michelle said, turning around to face where Jason's voice was coming from and putting her back to the bright sun. She squinted her eyes open as she acclimated to the light.

"You look nice and not the poster child for a CIA operative. I suppose you have hidden pockets in that dress?"

"Yes. I have a cell phone in one pocket and a tiny purse in the other. No weapons, so if there's any danger to this dinner, you'll have to do the shooting."

"Good to know, though I admit that other than a switchblade in my pants pocket, I'm not carrying any weapons either. I've been to the yacht club before to eat, and they're a tame and boring bunch."

"So, what's on the agenda tonight? Are you trying to impress someone or make an introduction or talk about your wind company? I want to be prepared to toss you any conversational softballs."

"I don't expect our suspect to show tonight. I'm just going to brag about my solar- and wind-powered boat, which won't impress the people at this yacht club. They only care about the size and speed of a boat."

"I did a little research before I came. Are you a member here?"

"No. The CIA has a yacht club membership near DC, and it has reciprocity with this club."

"You've admitted to working for the CIA?" Michelle asked in confusion.

"No, the CIA wisely controls that yacht club, so it gives us officers cover when we need it. They gave me a membership card in DC, and then the club here called and verified."

"Do you know much about sailing?"

"Fortunately, I grew up sailing, and though I haven't done much of it in the past decade or so, it's like riding a bike. I went out a few times before I left the East Coast just to refresh my mind. I'll sound like I know what I'm doing. In fact, if you have time to drop in during the daylight hours, I'll take you for a sail."

"I'd love to do that sometime, but I warn you that I'm a poor sailor. I get seasick easily, so it will have to be an extremely calm day on the water. Unfortunately, I'm using all my daylight hours to search locations. Maybe when my part of the job is no longer a race to visit all of these locations worldwide, I'll drop in and join you for a sail."

"Sounds like a plan. So let's go," Jason said, pointing to the route they needed to take to reach the clubhouse.

They had a great dinner and were waiting for their dessert to be served when Michelle saw Jason stiffen.

"What's going on?" Michelle asked, leaning across the table.

"Our suspect, David Niemi, just showed up to the bar."

EIGHT

"I thought you said he wouldn't be here tonight."

"I guess I don't know everything about him. I checked with the bartending staff and looked over video footage over the past several weeks, and he doesn't visit on Tuesdays. So I've actually not seen him in person despite my prior visits to this clubhouse."

"Do you want me to start a conversation with him? I could approach the bar and accidentally bump into him."

Jason shuffled through ideas in his head and nodded. He had a feeling that Michelle would get further with their suspect than he would. He watched her approach the bartender, then she moved lightening fast to bump Niemi's hand that was holding his drink. The drink and glass went flying, making a loud noise when it crashed on the floor and spilled its ice cubes and liquor contents.

"Oh my gosh, how clumsy of me. Can I buy you a new drink?" Michelle asked, meeting their target's eyes for the first time.

David Niemi was considered to be a fast thinker, but he was puzzled at how the woman had seemed to come out of nowhere and bumped the arm holding his drink. It took him a few seconds to focus on her question before he responded, "No, that is fine. Eduardo already has a new drink under way."

Michelle followed the direction of Niemi's hand to see that the bartender was indeed making a new drink.

"I'm sorry that caused you to make a new drink, Eduardo. I'm Michelle, and my darn shoes are making me clumsy," she said, holding out her hand to shake with Niemi. He was known to be a germaphobe, so Michelle was interested to see if he would shake her hand.

He did not. Instead, he introduced himself. "I'm David Niemi, a member of this club. Which boat are you with, Michelle?"

Damn, she forgot to pay attention to Jason's boat's name.

She felt a hand on her waist as Jason said, "She's with me aboard the Wind Century yacht. I'm visiting from the Capitol Yacht Club."

"Ah, is that the boat powered completely by the wind?"

"Yes. I've nearly reduced my carbon footprint to zero, but then, is that enough to avert the coming tragedy of climate change?"

Michelle reached up and put a hand on his chest and said, "Oh Honey, can't you just let go of that whole hot planet stuff? I'm tired of hearing about the evils of climate change."

She saw his eyes briefly blaze like he was trying not to laugh at her simpering review of climate change. Instead, he turned toward Mr. Niemi and said, "It's a point of contention between us. I think climate change is causing numerous disasters around the world, while she enjoys the sunshine."

Michelle wanted to kick him over his condescending attitude, but she gave him a sigh of disappointment.

David Niemi looked at Jason with renewed attention.

"I'm afraid I'm with your friend, Mr. . . ." he paused, realizing he didn't know the man's name.

"James Stout, CEO of Wind Century," Jason said, reaching out his hand for the customary business handshake.

"David Niemi, CEO of Einstein Industries. We make the all-electric car line, as well as batteries that your company probably uses to store the energy from wind," their target said, ignoring the proffered handshake.

"Well, we're sorry for butting into your evening. Nice to meet you," he said, smiling and turning away with his hand resting on Michelle's back so he could guide her back to their table.

They sat down, and Michelle whispered to Jason, "Where's my Academy Award?"

"You were so over the top I nearly gave away the whole operation. At least I now have my opening to sidle up to the man in the future."

"I think I like my assignment better. I travel the world looking for uranium centrifuges while you fake being a CEO and chatting up people at a yacht club. No thanks."

"I do envy you your role. It's so much more satisfying than mine. As a CIA operative, I've been shot, but I haven't been near death like you. It almost makes me wish I was . . . to come back with your special talent. Almost."

Michelle thought about telling him about her hometown of people with special skills and the fact she was genetically predisposed to have a special talent, but that would be breaking the code of silence regarding her hometown.

"Despite my newfound skill, I wouldn't wish nearly dying on anyone."

"Yes, it could have gone the other way," Jason murmured.

"Well, on that grim note, I'm off. I have an early schedule tomorrow. I have more caves and mines to explore." They had been walking back to Jason's boat, and so she gave a goodbye wave and disappeared before his eyes.

Seconds after she arrived home, she received a text from Jason: *Home safe?*

Yes, goodnight and thanks for an enjoyable evening.

Michelle fell asleep thinking about how boring the undercover job could be at times.

NINE

Michelle spent another fruitless day chasing mines and caves as potential enrichment locations. Other than the meth lab, three weeks of bouncing around the world had yielded the CIA nothing. She still had many locations to visit and decided to spend a few hours with the data analysts to see if she could narrow down the locations. She made an appointment and found herself sitting down with two analysts and her boss the next morning.

"Could we track his boat or plane to see where our suspect is moving about? If we had his cell phone location, we would know if he is focused on a location outside his usual travel routine. If he plans to destroy a good part of the world, I would think he would need to be somewhere safe himself, right? Suppose you're in the middle of a big city that comes to a screeching halt once its infrastructure begins to shut down without electricity generated by oil. In that case, you have a plan not to be there. You could die in a mob of Zombies."

"Okay, Michelle, there are no Zombies, but you make a good point that we would expect Mr. Niemi to hide out somewhere during the apocalypse. That somewhere would have power generated by wind, water, or sun."

"Yes, exactly. He would need a place to hide with a farm to create food, shelter, power, TV, etc. He's not going to go underground and live in a cave waiting for the world to die out while trying to stay away from the fallout of a uranium bomb."

"I've met our suspect, Mr. Niemi. I wonder if there is anything we can do to limit these locations more," Michelle pondered.

"Like what?" Meeks asked.

"What about his family? Surely he would want to take them with him?" said one of the analysts taking notes.

"He dumped his first two wives with whom he had six kids. His last divorce was about five years ago, and now his partner and he had a baby in the past year, I think," Meeks said.

"Exactly, I can't see him leaving behind all those children and the current partner. Perhaps even his parents. However, I would like to think that his parents aren't in on his plans if indeed those plans exist. They seem to be steadier people than the son."

"Okay, we'll see what we can find. I would think if I was the madman planning to blow up the world's oil reserves, that I would want to be on an island somewhere to wait out the world, and I'd have a big house to protect friends and family and a way to support them. While major population centers will be destroyed, there will be many small populations across the world and people who have off-the-grid power to support them through the tough times. It wouldn't be just Mr. Niemi's friends and family that survive. So how do we get data on where he's been traveling and what islands he owns around the world?"

"We've been searching records. Between hiding behind shell corporations and offshoring his actions, he's not that easy to trace. We've searched WikiLeaks and the Panama Papers. He's been a businessman for over twenty years and has a large family to hide transactions behind. Still, we're growing a list of properties. Here's the list of over ten properties he owns. Two of them are islands, and one is on the edge of a National Park in Montana. As near as we can tell from satellite pictures, there isn't another property around for fifty miles. I know this is slow going, but we're adding a property each day to the list."

"Does your list of properties show up on my list of places to visit?" Michelle asked.

"It does not. The list you're working on was compiled before we began to search for his properties. However, there may be some overlap. Give me a minute and I'll search," said the analyst.

There was silence in the room as occupants either tried to find the overlap of locations or tried to think of another way to better focus on where he might have built a bunker or otherwise substantiate that the billionaire was also a madman out to sabotage the world.

Michelle noticed that Meeks read something on her phone and smiled.

"Sheila, good news?"

"Depends on how you look at things. Remember the cave you checked out, and you said an explosion blocked the entrance? Well, a Colorado mountain rescue group used your cave as an opportunity to practice a cave rescue. They spent a few days moving boulders and discovered two men alive in the tunnel. They were taken to a hospital and observed overnight but have now been arrested for operating a meth lab. So the good news was they were rescued, but the bad news for them at least is they are going to jail."

Michelle smiled, "Personally, I think I'd rather be in jail than dead, so good news even for the suspects. Were they making something and it blew up?"

"No, it was bad luck. The ceiling randomly fell while the two men were inside the meth manufacturing area. If they had been on the other side of the collapse, it would have been no big deal, but they had no way to tell anyone they were trapped, and they figured they would just die."

"Oh well, karma has a way of settling scores."

"Indeed."

The analyst hit a button, and they heard a printer start up. Moments later, they were staring at a shorter list of seven locations.

"Okay, I'll begin visiting them later today. I almost want to find a stack of centrifuges if only to validate our theory. It's early enough in the enrichment process that we can put a stop to his plan."

"I hear what you're saying. I'm sure you're tired of visiting all of these places," Sheila Meeks said. She then looked at the analysts and asked, "How about mining uranium? Is there any indication he's doing that?"

"We've been tracking shipments from the major uranium mines worldwide. However, the quality of reporting from some countries is better than in others. Uranium gives off radiation, but short of flying unmanned planes over cargo containers or trains, there isn't a way to physically detect that there is uranium in a shipment."

"Okay, we'll see what you can do to find any unusual uranium shipments or purchases," Meeks said as she and Michelle stood up to leave the conference room.

Michelle stopped at the door as another thought came into her mind. "Does our suspect own any uranium mines?"

"Oh God," Sheila Meeks exclaimed. "We'll have to run that question through a bunch of officers in the know."

Michelle soon departed the office and headed home with a new list of potential places to inspect. Using her home computer and detailed maps, she plotted a new course for the next couple of days and sent her itinerary to Meeks before she headed out to the top destination on her list. It was an island in the Caribbean fairly close to Venezuela, location of the largest oil reserves in the world. If you were going to wage war on oil, then the first two targets had to be Venezuela and Saudi Arabia, which supplied thirty-eight percent of the world's oil.

She teleported to the small island close to Venezuela. She'd studied it through both Google Earth and CIA satellite images, and so she appeared exactly where she wanted to be. She was in a palm-tree edged rain forest. She was just north of the equator, and the weather was hot and humid. It was eighty-seven degrees, and Michelle could feel the sweat running down her back.

She spent her time getting her bearings. On a deserted island, one might think there would be no sound. Instead, she was bemused to hear birds and other animals cackling with vibrant conversations. She hoped that no snakes or crocodiles made the swim from the mainland, given the swampy jungle she was walking through. She knew by studying the map that the lone house on the island was about a half-mile to her north. She doubted that this was the island with the centrifuges as it appeared to be powered by gasoline generators, and she thought their suspect would need and want wind- and sun-powered electrical systems.

The island hadn't been explored as it was private property. The possibility of having caves was one of the things she would be looking at. Some Caribbean islands contained caves that were a must-see attraction for tourists. However, this was a small island, and Michelle didn't know if there was a high enough spot that might feature a cave. One of the things she planned to explore was to see if any cliffs ringed the island as that often was where caves were located. The island didn't have any other building big enough to house enough centrifuges to enrich uranium. At least that was what satellites showed. The island was about four miles by two miles, and she planned to explore it in its entirety and cross it off her list. She wondered if the island's inhabitants were on the island. She decided to teleport up to the house to take a quick look to know whether she could explore the island in the open and without being careful, or if her exploration needed to be done in secret.

She opened the images of the island on her phone as she wanted to get close to the dock but stay hidden. Michelle supposed the owners could come by helicopter, but there wasn't a helicopter pad or small runway on the island. That left a boat as the transportation source for the inhabitants. She studied the dock and planned to appear in the trees at the start of a small rainforest near the dock. A moment later, she was standing in the trees, staring at a somewhat shabby cigarette boat tied up at the dock. It might make for a rough ride across the ocean, but it was speedy. Okay, there were other humans on this island. Now she just needed to find them. Using the trees, she was able to make a circuit of the exterior of the house. No humans around the outside and none that she could see through the windows.

What to do next? The house was on a private island and therefore wasn't subject to permits. How could she find the floorplan if she wanted to pop inside the house? Someone must have the blueprint plans to build the house, even without permit approval.

It was the afternoon, and perhaps the inhabitants were at the beach. She again pulled up the pictures of the island as she remembered there was a sandy beach somewhere. She heard a noise and saw three men leaving the house and heading toward the boat. They were carrying things out of the house and placing them on the dock before going back inside the house.

She watched a while longer and smiled. These men weren't the owners. They were robbing the house and carrying out things that they could sell. Michelle debated taking a video of the men but decided the billionaire owner could afford the losses of the robbery. Also, she would have to explain the presence of the person shooting the video to the owner. Best just to hide her presence. At least she now knew that the island was hers to explore. She studied the photos again and headed to the cliff area of the island to search for a space large enough to hide a series of centrifuges.

She reached the cliffs, and there was a fifty to seventy-foot drop into the water. She wished she could use her skill to hover about the water as if she had on a jetpack, but her teleport ability didn't work that way. She peered at some offshore rocks, looking for one suitable for her to stand upon and not be knocked off by a wave. It would be a drag to teleport to a rock only to be hit seconds later by a wave that pitched her into the water. The water might feel refreshing, but the rocks underneath would be difficult to avoid.

She found the perfect outcropping that she was looking for and found herself standing there moments later. Before looking at the cliff, she took a moment to watch the ocean behind her to make sure she was in a safe location. Another rocky outcropping took most of the force of the waves coming at the shore, so she was good. She turned around and viewed the cliff with a pair of binoculars, looking for any openings. She could feel sweat rolling down her back in the afternoon sun, even with the ocean wind. She tried to remember the Siberian cold of a few weeks prior when she rescued Captain Cox, but that barely cooled her off.

She saw an opening that might lead into a cave. She wanted to explore it, but it could be a tricky move for her. She had no idea how tall the cave opening was, and the last thing she wanted to do was slam her head into stone. She took a seat on the rock. She imagined being inside the rocky opening in a seated position with the rock supporting her butt and her legs and facing out to the ocean. She was inside the cave a moment later, she heard a noise behind her as she apparently, had disturbed some cave inhabitants. She wondered if they were bats or birds. Something fluttered by her face as it left the cave, and Michelle was glad she was sitting down. She would have hated it if she reacted by falling out of the cave. After the animals settled down, she reached for her flashlight, rolled over onto her belly, and shined it inside the cave. That started a fresh wave of movement. It appeared the cave was small, with no more than another ten feet beyond her head. She teleported herself back to the offshore rock to look for other caves but found none. She gave one more look at the island and judged there was nowhere else to hide a uranium enrichment facility. Time to move on to the next spot.

The next location was a series of islands seemingly halfway between South America and the African Continent. It was a British Overseas set of islands. While deserted, they seemed very impractical. It was a long airplane flight or a six-day boat trip. The residents would notice if a private billionaire suddenly had multiple visitors by air or boat. Still, she planned to explore the island just to confirm her thoughts. The CIA was also checking flights to that location over the past six months. She thought it would be a quick visit to check the only location that included caves, and then she would move on to Greece tomorrow as it was already dark in that part of the world.

TEN

The next morning she dropped in on a Greek island called Apronisi Island, which Michelle found confusing. She had visited Santorini as a tourist and didn't recall seeing any nearby uninhabited private islands. She did a little research and found several islands close by that were governed by Santorini, so this island must be included in that political region. It appeared to be a big chunk of volcanic rock likely formed at the same time as the other three islands of Santorini. The rock was fairly flat on top with craggy cliffs all around. She was dressed in camo clothes the shade of the beige landscape she was standing on. If a plane flew over the island on approach to the Santorini airport, they hopefully wouldn't see a lone woman standing atop the island and try to rescue her.

Michelle used her teleport skill to move quickly around the flat top of the island. Then she moved on to the island's cliffs as she had noted from the satellite pictures that there appeared to be caves in the midst of the cliff's edge. She was about to go down to the area where a beach was located, but she saw an excursion boat approaching the island. This island was entirely too busy in a busy ferry area to be a secret uranium enrichment lab site. She needed to go home and study these locations better.

A moment later, she was back inside her condo in Virginia, studying the maps of the possible locations around the room. The cave that became a meth lab was a far better location than all of these islands she looked at. Either the islands were too far from the mainland or were in a busy lane of boat traffic that would notice a bunch of activity taking place as they installed the centrifuges. Besides, they had to have several dump truck loads of uranium ore rocks to enrich. There was no way a dump truck could get at some of these remote locations like the island off the tip of Venezuela in the middle of the Caribbean or even this small Greek island. She was back to thinking about vacant areas of the United States. There were large swathes of rural land in many states that would be perfect for hosting a uranium centrifuge facility, and no one would notice. She pulled up an aerial view of a uranium processing plant in New Mexico. The buildings looked to be the size of an American football stadium. So really, a cave was simply not big enough. She needed some big buildings in the middle of nowhere to be her mad billionaire's nuclear weapons lair.

Michelle pulled out her list of locations, looking for big buildings on large pieces of land, maybe near the Canadian border, to make it easier to drop a bomb on the Calgary oil and gas supply. She ran her finger down the list and found what she was looking for—a large property owned by their suspect in an area that would be convenient to sabotage Canada's oil reserves. She opened the weather app on her phone to see what the temperature was at the moment. She didn't want to freeze herself by appearing in Greek isle camo apparel rather than late spring snow apparel. She might find snow at the place she was going. She heaved a sigh of relief when she saw that the high was fifty degrees at the moment. She could add a warm jacket and go. The CIA analyst had picked this property as Mr. Niemi had owned it for a decade. He described it as a cattle ranch, and it consisted of miles of land for grazing and buildings to support the ranch.

She pulled up the most recent satellite images and could see a series of buildings that might house cattle in the winter or might house centrifuges now. She decided that was where she would teleport herself to—outside one of the buildings and hopefully not in the middle of trouble.

In the blink of an eye, she was standing outside the buildings she had viewed on satellite. She did a quick full circle to determine that no one was watching her. She then looked for security cameras as she didn't want to alert anyone to her presence. They were on the door, she saw as she peered around the corner, and quickly ducked out of sight. Now the question was how could she get inside to look around. She sniffed the air but didn't smell manure. That suggested there wasn't livestock in the immediate vicinity, and so why would a ranch need this extra-large warehouse/barn structure? Maybe there was an exotic car collection or WWII military tanks?

She could hear noise coming from inside the building, but fortunately, no one observed her arrival as far as she could tell. It was time for her to nose around—looking for uranium ore or a centrifuge or a huge stash of acid. Each of those items was required to enrich uranium. She looked around for windows but saw none. She moved to the other end of the building viewed a second door, again with a security camera. Did she dare to teleport inside the building? Without knowing what was inside, she could end up atop a moving or dangerous piece of machinery. She decided to chance it and try to teleport inside by imagining the inside of the door she could see at the back of the building. She could only hope that nothing was in her way.

Michelle closed her eyes against the afternoon Montana sun so she wouldn't be blinded by the building's darkness when she arrived inside. She opened her eyes to see another metal door in front of her. She glanced around and thought there was a metal framed wall as though there was a building within the building. If Mr. Niemi was up to no good, then this was the suspicious place. This was weird enough that she took pictures and teleported herself to CIA headquarters. She texted Sheila to make sure her office was empty, and then she left Montana.

As she popped into Sheila Meeks' office, her boss was startled by the appearance of her special operative.

"No matter the number of times I see you do that thing of teleporting in and out of the CIA, I'm still shocked by your appearance."

"I would be too. In fact, the time I teleported home to find Agent Smith sitting on my sofa, I had to put my hand to my chest for the shock of finding someone in my home. Hopefully, I never go home and pop in on a burglar."

"Ah, I wondered how he figured out what was going on."

"He picked my locks and waited for me to come home. He understands that keeping my ability a secret keeps me safe and alive. You can always pair me up with him for assignments going forward. I wanted to talk to you about what I'm thinking and what I see out in the world."

"Did you find something?" Sheila asked eagerly.

"Maybe, but I wanted to tell you about what I was thinking first. I visited multiple islands as I thought that if you were trying to do bad things, then a private island was a good place to hide."

"I would agree with that analysis."

"I was standing atop an uninhabited island near the Greek isle of Santorini. Tourist boats visit the beach, and people snorkel. There are caves in the sheer rock cliffs of the island, and I was going to target them for uranium enrichment."

"Sounds reasonable, so what's the problem?" Sheila asked.

"Santorini is filled with tourists, and cruise ships stop there.

There are ferries that go to other Greek islands. Uranium enrichment will require the delivery of dump truck loads of uranium ore. How are those dump trucks going to make multiple stealth deliveries of rock? Furthermore, I looked at a few uranium enrichment locations, and they are like three football fields in size. There's no cliffside cave that is going to be big enough for this process."

Sheila thought about Michelle's reasoning and nodded her agreement, "We thought of islands for secrecy and for a place to hide out while the world fell apart without fossil fuels."

"Yes, but think of the raw materials and size of the space required to make nuclear bombs. I think we can cross most islands off the list."

"So, where did you go looking, Michelle?"

"A large ranch in Montana. It is a vast acreage of land, and there are large farm buildings that make sense for livestock activities like milking, housing, etc."

"Okay, I see your reasoning. What did you find?"

"I approached the largest farm building on this ranch. There are cameras on the doors and no windows on the building."

"Aren't most barns solid wood? I don't necessarily recall seeing windows in the barns I pass."

"I don't disagree with that conclusion. I teleported just inside the door of the barn. You know that I must physically imagine what something looks like to be able to travel to the location. I didn't know what the interior of the barn looked like or what it was filled with. If there were cows inside, I didn't want to land on them or in a wet cowpie. With the cameras on the door, I didn't want to risk alerting whoever was monitoring them."

"So, what did you find?" Sheila asked, smiling at the image of landing in a wet cowpie.

"I found a metal wall. It appeared to me that a metal building was constructed, and then a wood barn was placed around it, so it fits with buildings in that region in case anyone was looking. There was just enough space at the entrance for me to turn around. Further along the wall, the space narrowed to nothing."

"That's odd. I grew up in the country and can't think of a single barn that was metal lined. Mostly because farming costs a lot of money and the last thing you would spend it on was an aesthetic exterior."

"Exactly what I thought. I also didn't smell any cow, pig, or goat products, nor did I hear any animal sounds."

"Were there people inside?" Meeks asked.

"None that I saw or heard. There were vehicles parked nearby, so it is possible that people were inside the building."

While they were talking, CIA Officer Sheila Meeks used Google Earth to focus on the piece of land where Michelle had sighted the odd building. She zoomed in on the barn and agreed with Michelle that it looked like any other barn that she had seen in the countryside except for the fact that it was newer.

"This ranch ended up on the list because it was owned by someone in Mr. Niemi's family?" Michelle asked.

"Yes. It's a trust named after his youngest child. He had an unusual name for that child–like Unit 251 or something. The trust owns the property."

"Do you know how long the ranch has been in his family's hands?"

"He bought the parcel five years ago and then transferred it to his child last year," Meeks said, glancing through a document on her desk.

"If he's worried that global warming will create a bad future for this child, it would make as much sense as anything else he does. Transfer ownership of a ranch from himself to that child, but also use it to fix the future climate problem for that child. Especially this child, as Niemi was almost fifty years old at the time the baby was born."

"Yeah, he was always a climate activist, but you're right that it's this youngest child that could live to 2100 and will be the one most affected by global warming. I'm going to request a few satellites to stay focused on that property so we can watch the traffic there. Is there a house on the property?"

"I didn't get that far. I just had the brainstorm about location when I was in Greece. I came home to my condominium and looked for something more like this property, and then I went after large buildings because if someone is going to install centrifuges, it needs to be a large building. It would make sense that he would have a house on the property as he and his family need a place to hang out while the world implodes. I would expect there to be many windmills or solar panels for when the world stops using oil for power. I haven't looked for either of those yet."

"I like your line of reasoning. I hadn't thought of the practicality of moving iron ore rocks, but I think you're correct that Niemi knows he has to work with the raw material rather than buy a more refined uranium product without the world noticing."

"So what do you want to do now? Should I head back to the land in Montana and explore further, or would you rather get satellite images? I could go explore other locations on the list."

"That's a good question," Meeks said, thinking about where to optimally place her intelligence officer where she could do the best job given her special talent.

"Have you heard anything from Jason? Is he making headway with Niemi? Do we have a sense of how many people it would take to handle this enrichment process? The machines are doing the work, but I would think there is something for a physicist to do while the centrifuges are running. Someone would have to take delivery of the rocks and crush them into a usable form. Do we have a report anywhere that says how big the operation needs to be?"

"I think we need another in-person meeting. I'll see if we can video conference Jason into the room. We have a small office in the San Diego area that should allow us to do an encrypted call. I'd like to get Tina McDonald and the analysts in the room so we can think about your logistics questions. We could then see if Jason can work that into his budding relationship with Niemi at the yacht club. I don't like the metal building within a barn, and I think you've thought of some good reasons to eliminate properties on the list. We need to discuss that and see if we have dump trucks visiting that property. I'll text you a time, but I think we're done for the day."

Michelle nodded and decided to head down to the gym and get in a good workout. This was the most time she'd ever spent continuously traveling around the world. It was both exhilarating and exhausting. It was fun to experience life in different parts of the world, but making sure her teleporting skills were never noticed made it a high-stress endeavor rather than a continuous string of mini-vacations.

ELEVEN

Apparently, Sheila Meeks had pulled all the appropriate strings, because all of the important people were in the room the next morning, and Jason was on a video screen. The poor man looked like he hadn't gotten enough sleep. It was early on the West Coast, and he might have been out late at the yacht club or socializing with someone related to this project.

Sheila had Michelle go over her thoughts about uranium enrichment facilities as she visited a couple of locations over the past week ending with her visit to the strange barn in Montana the previous day.

"Case Officer Watson, I agree with your analysis of locations. We should have thought of that at the time we compiled the list. Someone sells uranium ore online, and it's one-hundred dollars for a little more than three ounces. That is not enough to make a nuclear weapon with—you are correct that it will take dump truck loads unless our suspect has another source of a more purified product. For now, let's eliminate any location that can't be serviced by a dump truck," MacDonald said to the analysts.

"And the property in Montana?" Michelle asked.

"I grew up in a city in Iowa. Even though my family were not farmers, I spent a fair amount of time on farms in that state. It's not as cold as Montana, but it's close. I can't think of a barn I ever entered with a metal interior. Nor can I remember a farm without animal sounds and smells, but it's possible that he did away with his farm animals, given his focus on global warming. They fart a lot of methane which makes climate change worse. We've moved a few satellites to watch this property. We'll have more information in the next twenty-four to thirty-six hours."

"There are defunct uranium mines in Utah, Wyoming, and Colorado, making it easier to transport the rocks to Montana. Still, I can't see that no one would notice a caravan of dump trucks. It's close, but even one-hundred miles is a long distance to drive that kind of vehicle," said one of the analysts.

"Yes, I'd agree with that. Jason, any news from your angle?"

"I'm dining at our suspect's house tonight. I'll script in a conversation about large ranches. I read about energy generation at the North and South Poles, and they've installed wind turbines at the various outposts. Maybe I can pitch installing a wind farm on his Montana ranch. Is there a great electricity use to operate centrifuges? Could we check the electrical usage at the ranch?"

"Good question. Our suspect manufactures batteries that are used to store solar energy and so it makes sense that he would already have equipment in place to power his land. Especially if, indeed, he stops oil production worldwide," replied an analyst.

"I didn't see any windmills when I visited, but I hardly saw much of the land," Michelle added. "I think there is one other large ranch on the initial list, which I'll visit tomorrow. It's in the state of New Mexico."

"The land in New Mexico is owned by one of our suspect's companies. There are published reports that he was looking for tax breaks from the state to build a large battery facility on land that is of little value. In the end, he built his factory in Nevada where desert land is cheap and plentiful, and there is endless sunshine."

"So, we expect that land to be vacant, correct?" Michelle asked the analyst.

"It's listed on the county tax records as unimproved."

"Okay, I'll check it out. If you can forward me more satellite pictures of the ranch in Montana, I'll pay another visit there as well."

The analysts speculated in private about how Michelle moved around like she did. Most thought she had a secret private jet/helicopter that she was testing for the military. They could think of no other way she could visit a remote place in New Mexico and then Montana on the same day. The two destinations were at least one thousand miles apart. It would make a long day to drive from one to the other state, let alone get from Virginia to New Mexico all in a day. She had to have a supersonic jet and then a helicopter to move around. The analysts refocused on MacDonald as she was talking about the next steps.

"Remember, we don't have any evidence after nearly a month of searching that Mr. Niemi is involved in a plot to destroy the major oil fields of the world. We don't know if anyone is sick enough to try and wreak this much disaster and death on planet Earth. That said, if anyone has the money, brains, and sheer resources and moxie to do it, then it's our man, Mr. Niemi."

The room cleared out, and Michelle and Sheila headed back to her office. As they were walking, Michelle received a text from Jason:

Are you available to join me tonight for dinner at our suspect's house?

Yes. What's the dress code, and where and when should I appear?

California casual. Meet me on my boat at 5. It's early for dinner, but he said to come over at 6.

See you there at 6.

"I'm joining Jason and Mr. Niemi for dinner."

Sheila frowned and asked, "Is that a good idea? What if you're caught on some surveillance tape on one of his properties, and he recognizes you as Jason's dinner companion?"

"You forget I already met him"

"Oh, yeah, right. I'm starting to run short on sleep and it's only going to get worse."

"Yeah, remember, I spilled his drink and made a little scene to introduce Jason. It seemed to work well."

"Did I tell you last week that I don't like that you've met our suspect?"

"No, but I'm more careful than you can imagine making sure that I'm never caught on any video surveillance doing my disappearing act. I'm sure I wasn't caught yesterday when I visited the ranch in Montana. I know you're worried about the agency, but I'm more worried about staying alive. I don't want to leave any evidence of my teleport skill for the public to discover. All of America's enemies would put a target on my back to kill me given that I'm such an effective spy."

"I know," Sheila said. "I don't know if I've ever thanked you for making a choice to do good rather than bad with your skill. Within the agency, we planted information that you own or are somehow connected to a supersecret jet that moves you around the earth with speed. It's a top-secret military plane that you're testing for them."

"I figured the analysts just thought I was lying or using Google Earth to visit these locations. I like the agency's explanation as it somehow seems plausible."

"If you're going to risk this mission by meeting our suspect in person, we should at least give you some tools to leave behind. Let me call someone in our technology area. We'll outfit you with a few items to leave behind in our suspect's house. Do you have an outfit to wear tonight that contains many pockets?"

"No. I'll bring a purse in my backpack and wear cargo pants under or over whatever I find to wear tonight if I need additional space. Then I'll leave the purse behind with Jason but use it if there are any further meetings with suspects on the West Coast."

"Okay, I'll text you information of when we need you back here this afternoon to collect these gadgets. That gives you time to do more research on our suspect, load your backpack, and get a little more rest than you'll likely have in the coming thirty-six hours."

"Okay," Michelle said and disappeared before Sheila's eyes. As usual, she found herself staring into the empty space in which Michelle had been standing moments before.

Michelle arrived back at her condominium and spent a little time going through her closet to find a California casual outfit. What even was the style "California casual"? She brought up a software program and looked for pictures of what other people called California casual. Then she watched a street camera in Beverly Hills for about fifteen minutes to see what chic people walking out of a fancy designer store were wearing. From there, she picked clothes out of her dressing room—torn jeans, fancy top, covered with clunky jewelry, and a jacket. Yes, she looked like the hip women in Beverly Hills. She pulled a pair of cargo pants over the torn jeans to make sure she could zip the cargo pants up with the jeans underneath. She would have many pockets to hide whatever toys the CIA gave her to leave behind in Mr. Niemi's house. She checked the time and decided to follow Sheila's advice and get a little nap in as she might get less than six hours sleep tonight when she returned later and would still be on West Coast time.

Three hours later, feeling refreshed after a nap and a quick run around her neighborhood, she was back in the CIA building, being gifted with technology devices for her upcoming visit to their suspect's house. It was one of her favorite departments within the agency. There were nerds everywhere excited to explain the finer points of the toys they planned to give Michelle. She'd take about thirty devices with her, and she could plant them in his house, on his car if she came near it, and even his phone. They gave her this nifty tracking software that would tell the spooks at the CIA where the phone is traveling to and who is the person their suspect is chatting with. She just needed to be in Bluetooth range and for their suspect to avoid using his phone at the same time that Michelle was doing the download, or he would notice it.

She put the box full of devices into her car for the drive home. She dressed in her designer jeans and shirt, added outrageous jewelry, then pulled on the cargo pants. She began stuffing the pockets, and she was able to fit almost everything inside. She added a few devices to her jacket pocket, put on the backpack, and grabbed her cell phone and a transmitter for one of the devices, which she stuck in her bra. A millisecond later, she was standing inside the cabin of Jason's rental boat.

He was standing outside the room, not wanting to be in her way as she teleported to his boat. He was consumed by envy for such a cool skill. He watched her begin emptying her jacket and pants pockets. He smiled when she pulled a few more items out of her bra.

"You can never have enough pockets."

"HQ sent a bunch of devices with me for us to plant at Mr. Niemi's residence. I'll show you how the stuff works, and we can pick what to take," Michelle said as she began taking off the cargo pants. He'd wondered about the choice of the cargo pants when she first materialized as they hadn't seemed as chic as her usual dress. Now he understood.

She explained the various devices and went through how

each worked. For the critical devices—ones they wanted to tag Niemi's phone, computer, or person with, they each took one, not knowing who would be close enough to use the devices.

"Have you done this before? I haven't." Michelle asked.

"Yes, let's practice. I can't believe they planned to send you into the field without training. You could get caught and blow up the entire operation and be charged for illegal wiretaps or something. I've been doing this for years. Okay, did you notice that I placed one of the items in your pants pocket?"

"What?" Michelle asked, going through her pockets and finding the device inside a pocket, just as Jason claimed.

"Yes, when you're placing one of these devices, you need to move your target's eyes away from the hand dropping the device somewhere. Always have a visual distraction. So, I talked with my left hand while my right hand quietly dropped something in your clothing. Now try and do that with me."

Michelle smiled and moved so lightning fast that Jason wasn't sure what he was seeing.

"Check your back pocket."

Jason put a hand in his back pocket and found the same device he had planted in her pocket only minutes earlier. "Now I see why they didn't give you any training. You can move so fast that someone staring at you is left wondering what did my eyes just see?"

"It's a secondary teleporting skill that took me a little longer to understand and manage more than the major skill of moving around the earth."

"Speaking of earth, have you tried teleporting to the International Space Station?"

"No. I would definitely be on camera there, and my secret would be shared with too many people. Besides, I'm scared. What if I screw up and end up in outer space instead, and I can't breathe, and I can't get back to earth, and I die out there, and my body can't be recovered? Nope, not going to try it."

"You've really thought about this, haven't you? I suppose you've also not tried to land on an in-air jet or perhaps a submarine. Some locations feel unsafe," Jason said, thinking about how he would have explored such a talent.

"Besides, I was specializing in rescuing people from a variety of situations. I don't have enough knowledge to save an airplane or a submarine. I'm better at much smaller quantities of people."

"I wondered what you've been doing for the agency for the past five years. You have a unique skill that should be used in the right situation. The agency also needs to keep you a secret so no pairing you up routinely with other agents."

"Yeah, look what happened when I was paired with you, you figured it out. You're probably the only other CIA case officer I can be paired with—if everyone is as curious as you, my secret won't be one anymore."

"How do you keep the people you rescue from spilling your secrets? Surely they see you in action?"

"I use a combination of pressure and gratitude. I tell them no one would believe them, and they will end up in psychiatric care if they give away the details of their rescue. I also play on their gratitude for being rescued. I'm sure the agency comes behind me with more threats. Still, I have never again seen anyone I rescued, which helps with the thought that 'I was held hostage in solitary confinement. I saw this mirage of a woman help rescue me.'"

Jason was nodding and then thought of one more question, "What about your family? I thought I read somewhere that you have adult children?"

Michelle gave him a pained smile, "When I was recovering from my injuries, I told one of my kids, who are both married now, about my teleportation skill. They talked to my physician, concerned that I had brain damage. They didn't for one moment believe me. They have never seen magic at work. They visit me in my hometown, where I have a second home, in part because they love the retail businesses–bakeries, restaurants, wineries. My kids, like all outsiders, don't realize there's a little magic in all products. I decided it wasn't important for them to know of my talent. I may change my mind if one day they have children and those children have skills, but I don't think that will happen."

Jason nodded, reflecting on all she said, then he looked at his watch and said, "We better get going. We can talk more about our game plan on the drive to Niemi's house."

TWELVE

They decided they would play what they were–friends. As he drove through the busy LA traffic, Jason described what he had been up to with the fake business and the inroads he'd made into Niemi's inner circle.

"Have you discussed anything about climate change? Does he know you're passionate about it?"

"Yes. I've been reading some fringe articles on climate change and quoted them to our suspect. He seemed intrigued."

"When I was a cop, I never did undercover work as I am the poorest of actresses. My personality doesn't stretch much beyond who I really am. I can act the klutz on occasion, but that's the pinnacle of my acting ability. I'm good at my job of finding where our suspect might be building a nuclear bomb, and you're good at your job, which requires a great deal of acting to get into our suspect's inner circle. Kudos to Sheila Meeks for pairing us up on this assignment."

"I'll have to agree with your assessment. When I first heard about this assignment and researched my partner, I wasn't thrilled with your background. It seemed very bland, and I had no idea as we discussed the mission how you could be useful. I'm happy to say my judgment was very wrong. Let me tell you some of the fringe theories about climate change, so you don't look alarmed if we discuss them. By fringe, I mean the doomsday predictors who have climate change destroying the earth in the next five years."

Michelle's head turned quickly at Jason's last statement. "You mean to tell me that there are actual people who believe we are all going to burn up five years from now? Don't get me wrong by that question. I do agree that the earth is heating up, and that has all kinds of consequences. From what I understand of the situation, though, we won't all be dead in five years."

Jason nodded, "That's my assessment too. Let me tell you a few of the theories."

When he finished, Michelle asked, "Have you tested any of these with our suspect?"

"I have. I've gone so far as to disparage anyone wasting energy, and I've done some wishful thinking about powering the world with the wind. It's part of my persona as the Wind Century CEO."

"I'm glad you reminded me about that. I have to remember to call you James Stout. I'll look at you and think beer."

"Beer?" Jason said with puzzlement.

"Stout is a type of beer, and thinking about beer will help me remember to call you by a different name."

"You're not cut out for this undercover work. I'll be mouthing beer to you all night long just to keep you on task to call me James." They both laughed at this, although Jason was seriously worried.

They pulled up to an enormous, gated house, and Jason spoke into an intercom. The gate swung open, and they parked on a circular driveway.

"Either we're early, or this is a small social function,"

Michelle commented, seeing no other cars parked on the driveway.

Jason shrugged, and they got out of the car to walk to what appeared to be an eight-foot-tall door. He was carrying a bottle of wine, and he reached with the other hand for the doorbell.

"Why would you need a doorbell when you have an intercom at your gate?" Michelle wondered, as they heard the bell inside the house.

Jason shrugged but didn't say anything.

Seconds later, their host opened the door.

"Welcome, James," and then he looked at Michelle and narrowed his eyes while holding out his hand. "I think we met before, but I'm sad to say I don't remember where."

"Hello, Mr. Niemi. We met when I accidentally spilled your drink at the yacht club," Michelle said, giving him her best smile.

"Ah, yes. Call me David. Mr. Niemi seems too formal."

He took Jason's proffered wine, led the way to an outdoor patio, and directed them to a seating area. A maid arrived to take their drink orders and returned quickly with them as well as personal platters of appetizers.

They had a wonderful meal in a beautiful setting, but Michelle had a hard time relaxing enough to enjoy it. She was nervous about calling Jason "James." She was thrilled when Jason said they needed to head home as Michelle had an early flight out of LAX the next morning.

After more desultory conversation, they were heading down the driveway to the gate. They chatted about her fake trip for about a mile when he said he was pulling into a pharmacy for some acetaminophen as he felt a backache coming on. They did indeed pull into a pharmacy parking lot, but Jason went around to the engine compartment and released a wand taped inside the hood. He ran it over the car and found no listening or tracking devices other than the ones they had in their pockets and

Michelle's purse. He tossed the wand into the back seat, and they continued the drive to the marina and his boat, free to talk.

"What did you think? Is he planning on bringing an apocalypse to the world?" Jason asked.

"I don't know. I think historically, the most insane of horrible criminals had long periods of normalcy. They hide in plain sight and somehow keep a grip on their sanity while in public. He was capable of discussing the planet heating up in five years instead of instantly discarding the idea."

"Yes, but he didn't agree with the idea."

"True, but he did say we would be in a terrible place in twenty years just as his youngest child enters adulthood."

"Is that what he said, or was he just trying to have a rich discussion? I heard him mention the twenty years, but something about the way he said it made me think he was debating for the sake of debating without taking a side. Maybe I've been hanging out with the yacht club folk too much. They're a weird bunch."

"Maybe. Working your way into our suspect's inner circle seems like a painfully slow way to validate whether we have a real problem happening with this guy. Did the agency ever identify the source of the rumor? I mean, I don't think it takes a genius to develop this idea—I understand how to enrich uranium. I could set up centrifuges, spin it forever, then mix it in with a firework and throw it off a cliff and see what happens. I could watch enough videos on YouTube or visit the dark web to figure out how to build a bomb. You don't have to be a rocket scientist on this one, so maybe we should be looking at other suspects."

"You make a good point. Where are you going tomorrow? Maybe we can set up an early meeting before you head off to the other ranch in New Mexico. We can huddle with Meeks and see if there might possibly be other suspects who should be on our list," Jason suggested.

"I'm supposed to be off to New Mexico and then Montana,

but really I could leave much later than I am. The analysts think I fly a super-secret fast plane for the CIA."

Jason grinned, "Adds to your mystique. On the surface, it seems like there is nothing special about you other than you've been able to rescue people, but you must be the source of gossip and speculation."

"I like that word *mystique*. I'll work on using that for a cover for my teleport skill."

Jason checked the time and said, "I can pull over, and you could teleport to the boat to grab your cargo pants, then head home to Virginia. You'll get home about thirty minutes faster."

Michelle thought about his offer and nodded, "You don't have to pull over. I teleported off a snowmobile in Siberia just before it crashed into a military truck. That was my last assignment."

"You lead such an exciting life, Michelle. I'm envious of how easily you can get out of jeopardy with your skill. You would think the CIA would want you everywhere at once." Shaking his head, he bid her "goodnight."

"Goodnight," she replied and disappeared into the ether.

THIRTEEN

Jason had arranged a video call with Sheila Meeks at six the next morning in his time zone before Michelle left to explore. She thought about doing the call from New Mexico, but there was likely no cell service where she was going. She delayed her departure to talk to their supervisor about their suspect, David Niemi and to hear what intel the satellites had gathered on the Montana ranch.

"How did your dinner go last night? Any thoughts about our suspect?" Sheila asked.

"I don't know what to think. Niemi is smart, and he's concerned. It wasn't enough of a conversation for me to decipher his intentions," Michelle said. "Of course, Jason has spent more time around him, so maybe he has a clearer impression, but with my years of experience as a cop, there was nothing overall in his presentation that screamed 'I want to murder most of the world.'"

"Back to the original intelligence with this case, why was the focus on Niemi?" Jason asked.

"The CIA routinely monitors the sale of items related to the production of nuclear weapons. We saw a purchase of the raw materials to make enrichment centrifuges and an uptick in uranium mining. Mining has been declining since the mid-1980s as more nuclear power plants are taken offline," Meeks said.

"So why are we focused on Niemi as opposed to any other billionaire?" Michelle asked.

"The CIA monitors nuclear terrorism worldwide. Rumors have been increasing that someone was building such a weapon. There were a few other odd clues that caused our analysts to arrive at David Niemi."

"I'd think you would be chasing down rumors of nuclear bombs all the time."

"I believe the agency spends a fair amount of time doing that as we're more worried about foreign terrorists than domestic. We collect data routinely on anyone purchasing the components of nuclear bombs. Guess how many pounds of weapons-grade enriched uranium were stolen last year."

"Two-hundred fifty pounds," Michelle suggested.

"Wrong. Nineteen pounds over twenty years. Guess how many pounds you need to make a bomb."

"At least one-hundred?"

"Good guess, you're correct."

"So maybe we shouldn't worry about this as it seems so far-fetched," Jason said.

"Unless you look at David Niemi. He has so many more resources than any terrorist roaming the world. He has the manufacturing smarts to make his own. He knows how to buy uranium ore; he has many houses to hide the enrichment process, and he has a motive with his young child. We looked at a list of other billionaires and evaluated each for nuclear manufacturing capability. Then there's the final piece of evidence."

"Which is?" Jason asked.

"He's put most of his houses up for sale across the world

except for the Montana property. With a total of seven children, why would you sell all of your properties?"

"Maybe he's in financial trouble," Michelle suggested.

"No, we checked that. Niemi is flush with cash, and he's got a legal agreement with his current partner."

"Do any of his companies need money? Maybe they're starting a new project that takes lots of cash? Okay, moving on, there are apparently enough circumstances for him to come on the agency's radar screen. So I'll go back to searching for his centrifuge hidey-hole," Michelle said.

"I'm going to back off Niemi, but I'll discuss some outlandish climate change articles with folks at the yacht club. This is a slow and painful operation," Jason said. "I hope it's worth it in the end."

"This might be the most important operation in my career. If we're wrong, we don't want to slander or otherwise damage Mr. Niemi. If we're right, we need to save the world," Sheila said, looking down at her phone. She paused a minute to read something and then looked up. "The satellites showed a few employees showing up to the barn, but no animals have been seen near it. There are a few cows, horses, and goats in another part of the ranch. Not a lot of them but likely enough to feed the family for a while as the world goes dark without oil."

"How about the metal-lined barn? Any activity there? Anyone going inside?" Michelle asked.

"The analysts are still going over those buildings. They saw men and women enter and leave. However, no one is getting into a car and driving away. Some of the other buildings nearby must be for staff. We'll know more by tomorrow."

"Okay, I'm off to New Mexico, and then if the analysts can tell me which building they are going to, I'll check it out. Ask them to send me an exterior picture."

"Okay. Safe travels," Sheila said, and Michelle stood up to

head out to the parking lot and her car. It was good for the staff to see her arriving in a car. It added validation that she commuted like everyone else and likely helped keep the idea that she had a secret plane that took her on big journeys.

Sheila was left staring at Jason. "What's your gut reaction about Niemi? You have been around him more than any of us."

"He seems like your average annoying rich guy. Things go his way a lot, and he forgets to always be grateful for his good fortune. I've been trying to see behind the mask to see what's underneath, but it's hard to reach. It doesn't help that I'm portraying a fanaticism about climate change that I don't mostly believe myself. I guess I have trouble believing that anyone wants hundreds of millions of people to die. What kind of rotten core do you have to have to feel that the ends justify the means, and if you are that rotten, I should be able to sense it, I would hope. Maybe the listening devices that we left behind at his house will show something. It was too bad we didn't get close enough to his cell phone to put a tracer on it."

"Fanaticism is strange. I've seen perfectly rational people go nuts over something. I'll stand off to the side and ask myself, what made the person believe such an off the rails conspiracy theory? I guess there's something we're all passionate about that makes us a little crazy. In my position at the CIA, we certainly see entire countries elect an awful leader. Take North Korea-as a country, it has lagged far behind its southern neighbor to the detriment of its people. Suppose Michelle can confirm something unusual is going on at the Montana property today. In that case, we can move forward in a different direction. I will pull you out of the Southern California assignment and have you pair with Michelle in Montana. I'll think of a cover story to explain why you're sailing your boat back to Virginia so we don't raise suspicions from Niemi."

"And if Michelle doesn't find proof at the Montana location? What's your plan?"

"I don't have one yet, other than to hope that something comes from one of the devices you left behind. Did Niemi say when he was moving out of that house?"

"He didn't, and from his conversation, it seemed like he has reasons to stay in the area. Maybe he's taking possession of a yacht to live on or something."

Sheila nodded, and they ended the video call shortly after that.

Michelle pulled into her garage and was soon in her kitchen, checking the weather for the locations she needed to visit today. New Mexico would be warmer, and as far as she knew, she was visiting vacant land. She picked clothing that matched the landscape of New Mexico's high desert terrain. She checked her pockets for a gun, cell phone, small binoculars, a wallet, and a bottle of water. Even though she had used her talent thousands of times, there was always a tiny worry about getting back home—thus the bottle of water. It was rather silly on her part at this moment. She had had no doubt that her teleportation skill would work just before she smashed the snowmobile into the truck in Siberia. It was just that empty, wide-open spaces made her feel a little lost, like she wouldn't make it home again. She shook off her glum thoughts and folded up her map of the area she would be visiting. If her phone had no reception, she wanted a paper map as backup.

She'd imagine a plot of land in New Mexico, and now she was standing on it. There were hills all around and mountains farther away. The ground was covered with a boring green plant, and there were few trees. She could see snow on the higher elevation. There was no sign of humanity, no cars in the distance, and no sound but the sheer noise of the wind.

She moved around the property looking for buildings, but she couldn't find any structures. Then she moved around the hillside looking for caves that might contain the centrifuges, but there were none. She wondered then if the property could be mined for uranium ore. She'd been all over the large acreage and hadn't found evidence of a mining operation which would be hard to hide.

Michelle crossed this New Mexico property off her list of potential locations. That left Montana. She would head home, grab some different tools and warmer clothes, and see what she could find there. She was hoping to make her way beyond the metal wall to the interior of the barn, or else she planned a visit to the bunkhouse to see what kind of employees they were. Was there any identification laying around that would help her discover their identities? She was planning to use her teleporting skill to get inside the metal room, even if she had to imagine a long row of centrifuges to do so. She just hoped that her imagination took her inside the barn in Montana and not some place in Iran enriching uranium.

March in Montana meant that the weather fluctuated between cold winter and early spring. You really needed to check it frequently to guess what was going on. She was pleased to see it was snowing. Spring snows occurred at warmer temperatures, so the snowflakes were big and fluffy, which was perfect for hiding her appearance. She changed into a white and tan-colored outfit, tucking her hair inside a beanie. She carried the same stuff in her pockets as she had for New Mexico but replaced her water bottle with some hand warmers if it was colder than she expected.

Shortly, she was staring at the fir tree in front of her. She spotted this fir tree on her last visit and thought it would provide some cover as she examined the scene. She did her usual full circle turn and saw no one around. Without farm animals to take care of, why would anyone be out and about in this weather? She looked around for cameras using the binoculars, first examining the ones she had located before on the previous visit near the two barn doors. Then she moved her focus over to another building she now thought was staff quarters. She could see cameras there too. What ranch in remote Montana installed security cameras over all the doors? She wondered if any cameras were hidden in the trees; certainly, she would have lots of cameras around if she was making enriched uranium.

She spent at least fifteen minutes searching for additional cameras. All of a sudden, she heard a male voice behind her. How had she not noticed someone behind her? She had been concentrating on the view through her binoculars. What should she do? Give him a chance to fatally shoot her or just immediately disappear?

She was gone in a blink of an eye. She moved to another fir tree some distance away. She watched the man and checked her surroundings. She didn't want a second man searching for her. The man was searching in the branches of the tree she'd been standing behind like she had disappeared into them. That made her smile for a moment, then she thought of the seriousness of the situation. She looked to see if he was carrying any weapons. He had a gun in his hand, and who knew what under the bulk of his winter jacket. Michelle concluded that you didn't approach a woman in the snow with a gun unless you were up to bad things. She smiled again as the man was looking for footprints in the snow. There was no trail to the tree she had been standing at as she hadn't walked there. The fact that she disappeared and had left no tracks in the snow was puzzling the man. He did one more look around and then pulled out a cellphone and made a call. She debated briefly about getting closer so she could hear what he said. She opted for a tree much closer to him but behind and hoped that the sound would carry back to her.

The snowstorm was picking up with the wind making more noise. Michelle picked up a few sounds he said into the phone. It sounded like a foreign language. She pressed *record* on her phone and hoped that the words made sense when she listened to it later.

She continued to look around, wanting to make sure that she wouldn't be caught by surprise again. She could move fast and take the cellphone, but a wise man would cancel the phone and track where it was taken. She watched a while longer and then came up with a brilliant solution. She would grab his phone, disappear, and duplicate it with one of the devices the CIA had given her to copy Niemi's phone. Then she would reappear around the edge of the barn and toss the phone toward one of the barn doors. That way, she would get the contents from the phone, but it would look like the man was hallucinating if he talked about seeing a woman or that she took his phone.

She followed through, doing exactly what she planned. She teleported herself inside her condo, copied the phone, and tele-ported herself back to the edge of the barn, and tossed the phone. The man was still searching the trees where he had been talking on his phone. The good thing was that he hadn't run inside to have the phone tracked during its brief disappearance. She was back in Virginia in the blink of an eye. It was time to call Sheila Meeks.

"Sheila, it's Michelle. Let me tell you what's been going on today. I explored the New Mexico property and could find no evidence of inhabitants or mining. There were no structures on the property, and I saw no evidence of holes in the ground denoting uranium mining. After a change of clothes, I headed out to Montana. I was looking for additional cameras near that barn structure when I heard a male voice behind me though I couldn't say what the words were. I disappeared to another tree close by and watched the man. He carried a gun in one hand and looked through the tree branches where I had been standing. Then he used his phone to call someone. I moved closer behind a different tree, but the snow was picking up, and it was hard to hear over the wind. I tried to tape his conversation and then decided to change strategy. I grabbed the phone out of his hand and took it to my condo, where I duplicated it. I then went back to Montana and dropped it close to the barn door. This all occurred in under three minutes, and he was still looking for me when I returned and put the phone near the barn door. Should I bring the recording of the conversation and the phone's contents to you now?"

"Wow, you had an interesting day. I think you played it right. If you had a conversation with the man, it might've given him time to shoot you. Perhaps he's telling himself right now that he never saw you given the snowstorm and the fact that his cell phone is back with him and you're nowhere to be found. I would like to see what's on the phone and see if our analysts can figure out the language he was speaking. Something is going down at that barn for them to have that kind of security."

"Exactly what I thought. Who approaches a woman in a snowstorm with a gun in their hand? He was definitely not an upstanding citizen. Is your office clear?"

"Yes, but my assistant is outside, and she'll wonder where you came from if you didn't walk by her desk. So I'll send her out on an errand and text you when the coast is clear. See you soon."

Michelle did a quick wardrobe change, and when she received Sheila's text, she took herself to her supervisor's office.

FOURTEEN

Michelle appeared in Sheila's office and handed her the copy she made of the man's phone and the recording of his conversation on a zip drive. Sheila invited her to accompany her to a technology room where the nerds could figure out the phone copy and the language the man was speaking. Perhaps that would give them a clue as to where he came from.

"We've recently confirmed that our suspect still owns this property, correct?" Michelle asked.

"We haven't, but we'll do so now."

They watched as the analysts using headphones listened to the recording that Michelle made. They moved a variety of levers and listened to the voice over and over. Finally, they took off the headphones.

"He's speaking French."

"French? Usually, I'm pretty good at hearing that language. Are you sure?" Michelle questioned.

"Yes, although I don't believe he is a native speaker of French."

"Any guess as to what his native language might be?" Sheila asked.

"Might be English, but we'll send this to our linguistic department to have them decipher the accents."

"Were you able to cut out the sound of the wind? It was starting to snow pretty hard, and it was difficult to hear over the wind."

"We have software that we can use to remove background sounds. The trick is telling the computer what is the background sound versus the human sound that we actually want to hear. Still, the remaining sounds didn't make complete sentences. So we'll listen to it a few more times and give you as many words as we thought were said. The software says the language is French."

Sheila nodded and said her thanks, and the two women moved on to where someone else was wearing headphones and fiddling with the zip drive.

"Have you been able to trace the calls that were made on the cell phone?" Sheila asked the technician.

"Most of them. There are international calls on the phone which can be a little more difficult to track."

"Our linguistic experts said the man was speaking French with a non-native accent. Tell me more about the international calls. Maybe that will give us a clue as to the man's identity."

"OMG, I could have gotten more information off that phone," Michelle said, slapping her palm against her forehead. "I should've looked for fingerprints on the home button and where he was gripping it when I saw him. I can't believe I missed that opportunity. Maybe when this case is over, the CIA can put me through spy school."

The technician fiddling with the phone squinted up at Michelle and said, "Spy school?" But the look in his eyes said *I can't believe you just used those words.*

"That would have been good information to have although he may be from outside the United States and therefore his fingerprints would be harder to track, so don't beat yourself up too much. Besides, you were likely worried that the man would shoot you. I'm happy you were able to get away with a few martial arts moves," Sheila said.

"True, I was worried about the gun. It's not an everyday occurrence for me to be out in a snowstorm and have a man appear suddenly holding a gun."

"Didn't they see you drive up?" the technician asked.

Sheila and Michelle looked at each other, and then Michelle said, "The agency dropped me off from a helicopter about two miles away. I traveled the remaining distance using a battery-operated fat tire bike, and then the copter picked me up again when I was on the run. My bike has a rake off the back that covers my tracks as I pedal."

"Sounds cool," said the technician distractedly. "I think I've got everything off the phone. I was able to un-erase a few voice-mails. There are a few contacts saved on the phone by initials only."

"Okay, send me a list of the contacts and calls and whom they belong to as soon as possible," Sheila said, and she and Michelle exited the lab. "Let's go back to my office."

Once they were behind Sheila's closed door, she said, "We have many smart people working for the agency. I'm worried about your personal safety if our staff start trying to figure out how you move around."

"Would you believe the way I move around if you hadn't seen it for yourself?"

"No."

"Good. I don't think most people could believe in my teleportation skill if they haven't seen it. Certainly, as a cop, we were taught to collect physical evidence, which is something they don't have on me. It is why I drive my car here on occasion. Just in case someone is speculating about my activities. I do think it would help to have a script, though. Maybe I'll invent an obscure martial arts talent that allows me to defend myself. Jason said some people think I'm testing a top-secret plane that can land and take off vertically but flies at supersonic speed. I'll keep perpetuating that idea as a way to explain how I move around so fast."

"I hadn't heard that rumor about you. What have you been saying to the people you have rescued?" Sheila asked, now aware that there was a group of people Michelle had exposed her skill to.

"I ask them to stay silent on my skill. If they choose to talk, the agency will have them labeled mentally ill from their captivity, and they'll be locked up inside a psychiatric hospital. It's a fake threat, but if you say that to someone being held in captivity, it's almost worse than a death threat as they know firsthand how it feels to be imprisoned."

"Makes sense; good thinking on your part."

"I don't feel good saying it, but I think of the people in the future that I can help as long as my talent stays hidden from the world."

"Okay. I had a few moments of panic back there in the lab. You've had longer to think about it than I have, so let's work on that script when this assignment is over. Now, let's go back to Montana and discuss what we're going to do there," Sheila said, looking at her watch. "Darkness should be arriving there in about an hour. Should we send you back?"

"I haven't made it inside that barn yet. I also don't understand how I was spotted outside. Did I trip a camera or a motion sensor? Was it bad luck on my part? Since the guy had a gun in his hand, I must have been spotted on a camera. Wouldn't you agree?"

"Yes, I agree. Some of our spy satellites are getting more sophisticated. Perhaps we can see if they can locate Bluetooth transmissions coming from the woods around the barn. I hate to send you back there and have the guys locate you quickly again. I'd rather the guy be confused about who you are, where you went, and if you were actually there to start with. Why don't you head back to your condo and wait for word of what the satellite guys can do to collect more information on the property?"

"Okay," Michelle said, and then she thought of another idea. "Look, why don't I wait for darkness and go visit the building? I'll imagine the inside the metal barn and teleport there. I'll turn around quickly from the metal wall as that is what I'll be facing, take a look around, and come right back here."

"Have you ever timed how fast you can appear and disappear?"

"No, why?"

"I'd like to know our timeline for you to get in and out of a space before someone can shoot you dead."

"Let's do it right now and find out. I'll head to my condo, reappear in your office, do a 360-degree turn, then pop back to my condo, then come back here. You can time it with a stopwatch."

"Okay. Go."

Michelle vanished, reappeared, vanished, and reappeared again.

"How much time elapsed?"

"Less than two seconds. That makes me feel better. I think it would be hard for someone to pull their gun and shoot you in that little time. The first thing they would do is question what they were seeing before pulling a gun and shooting."

"So I should head over to Montana and be back in a few seconds?"

"Yes. If nothing illegal is going on inside that barn, we need to keep moving and look at the rest of the locations on the list. If something illegal is occurring, we will need time to marshal our resources. We would send an agency strike team to that location, and we need time to get them there. If you visit that barn now, we can get the strike force going within the next ten minutes. It will still take time to travel to Montana, so they would arrive there around midnight or so."

Michelle nodded and imagined the inside of the metal building based on what she'd seen on the outside. In the blink of the eye, she was in Montana with a nondescript metal wall in front of her face. She quickly turned around, scanning the room, and was gone again before any of the occupants could react if they had seen her. Michelle was pretty sure that no one had captured her quickie visit to the metal building.

She appeared back in Sheila's office with a look on her face that said it all.

"You found it! You found the illegal uranium enrichment facility."

"I did. I don't think anyone was looking my way when I made the quick visit."

"How many people were inside the building?"

"I saw three people, but that wasn't a thorough search of the building's interior."

"What did the building's inside look like?"

"It looked like a large room. It was filled with centrifuges like the ones I saw in the pictures. The employees working there were wearing white hazardous materials suits with their hair and limbs covered and a mask on. Should we discuss these findings with anyone else before I finish describing things for you?"

"Yes, let me see if I can get Jason and MacDonald on a call. I was hoping the rumor was false, but it's clearly not. Hold on while I make a few calls."

True to her word, she had a video conference organized a few minutes later. Michelle, Jason, and Sheila were on a video screen while MacDonald phoned in from somewhere.

"You have news?" asked MacDonald. "My assistant said this was urgent."

"Yes, Michelle Watson stepped inside the metal building in the barn. As we feared, it was filled with centrifuges."

"Just a moment." There was silence on the line, then the Assistant Director came back on the line. "I'm on my way back to Langley. I will try and get my brethren from the FBI to head over from the Hoover Building. We need to plan our next steps. I'll see you soon in a conference room that my assistant will find," and then they heard the sound of a phone disconnecting.

"Should I head to the airport for a flight to DC?" asked Jason.

"Not yet. We may still use you in LA. A few hours won't make a difference. Besides, we might send you to Great Falls and have you meet Michelle there."

"Is that the closest airport to this ranch?"

"It is, but it still almost one-hundred miles away."

"Good to know. Should I sign off now until everyone reassembles in a conference room?"

"Yes, I'll dial you in perhaps thirty to sixty minutes."

There was silence in the room as Sheila and Michelle looked at each other.

"If an FBI person joins our meeting, I'll have to explain how I got from Montana to Virginia in record time. Perhaps it would be better to leave me out of the room and just say that agents on the ground found the centrifuges."

"Yeah, the CIA has no desire to reveal your special skills. MacDonald will want to hear from you directly, but there is something to be said for keeping you away from this meeting," Sheila said.

"Okay, I'll wait to hear what you both decide. Do you have any idea about when we can expect MacDonald?"

"No, but I will ask."

"Should I head back to Montana and grab a picture of the interior?"

"Good question. I would love a picture of the interior, but not at the expense of your life. You can't teleport with a cell phone in your hands, correct? It has to be in your pocket."

"Yes, but if I teleport with my hand in my pocket, it will take milliseconds to pull my hand out and snap a picture, drop the phone back in the pocket, and disappear. I think I'm safe, especially as the workers had their backs to me looking at something in front of them."

"Okay, let's send you back. Make sure your phone is on mute, and the flash is turned off."

"Good reminder. I'll also set it on the camera function, so I don't have to fool with the passcode," Michelle said while checking the settings on her phone. "If I have time, I'll shoot some video of the room."

"Don't be careless, and don't get caught. Stay safe."

Michelle nodded and disappeared into thin air. Sheila set her stopwatch running so she would know exactly how long Michelle was gone. She knew she would be in a state of panic until her most valuable asset returned unharmed.

The clock was approaching ninety seconds when MacDonald entered her office. Sheila waved her away, knowing that Michelle would be coming back.

"Move out of the way. Michelle is returning any moment."

Her stopwatch hit ninety-eight seconds, and Sheila was in a full state of terror when Michelle reappeared in front of her.

"What took you so long? Those were the longest ninety-nine seconds of my life."

"The workers' backs were turned away, so I took additional time with the video," Michelle said.

"You have a video we can all view?" MacDonald asked, eager to watch.

"Yes. Look at this," Michelle said, showing the two other women first the pictures, then the videos she took.

"So, the rumors are true. Someone is going to blow up the oil reserves of the world. I thought this was a wild goose chase at the start of this assignment."

FIFTEEN

An hour later, a large meeting took place at CIA headquarters. Meeks and MacDonald agreed to excuse Michelle from the meeting, especially as she had supplied them with the evidence in the video. It might become hard to explain how she shot a video in the evening in Montana, yet she was now in Virginia. Michelle was content to be excluded as that meant that no one would think to ask questions about how she returned from Montana so soon to hand over the pictures, among other questions. She checked the weather in California, thinking about returning to her home there, but she wasn't in the mood to relax. She had discovered a ticking timebomb that would turn the world upside down if deployed. She had the desire to head back to Montana and watch while the leadership decided on a strategy.

Could she perch in a tree and watch the barn but stay out of the range of cameras? It was dark there now. Would darkness hide her? What was the weather like at the moment? Had they seen her on a camera earlier, or did they use infrared that would find her body heat? Had she tripped a motion detector?

Her phone rang, which made her jump. She saw from the caller ID that Jason was calling.

"I thought you were included in the meeting?" Michelle said upon confirming it was Jason.

"I think this is such an overwhelming awful idea, that small fry like you and I are excluded from meetings. I think the President might even have joined this meeting."

"Wow! That's pretty cool to think that my pictures are being seen by the President."

"So why didn't they include you? After all, you found the site, and you would think they'd want first-hand knowledge."

"We've had some awkward moments at HQ as people try to understand how I move around so fast. It's not that they're curious or even devious. Their minds can't seem to help trace the path and give me the squint eye for telling the truth about where I've been. Sheila and I decided for this assignment to avoid meetings for me with outsiders. I don't mind, and I do appreciate that Sheila recognizes that the secret of my talent is critical to my staying alive. However, this is a world-ending apocalypse from a nut-job billionaire. I was just thinking about heading back to Montana to watch over the site. I mean, what if they move stuff out? I realize we can't just send the local sheriff there and arrest everyone, and probably the agency is watching the facility from the sky, but I feel like we need boots on the ground."

"Tell you what. Let's both go rogue. I'm in Salt Lake City changing planes for Great Falls. I'm supposed to be there in an hour. Can you meet me at that airport with a rental car, and we'll drive to the ranch?"

"Seriously? You really are going rogue. Sheila Meeks asked you to stay in Los Angeles. Why?"

"Same reason you're thinking about heading there. We seem to be the only two humans on earth worried about the here and now while our bosses develop a grand plan on what to do. Hopefully, they won't be too late."

"I was planning on teleporting into a tree and hanging out there and watching, but you can't do that. How are you going to get onto the property without being seen? We disconnected the call before you heard, but I had a man approach me where I was standing in the trees in a snowstorm with a gun in his hand. They have some kind of surveillance on that property. I don't know if I was caught on camera or infrared, or if I tripped a motion detector."

"Crap. I'll think about that on the way there. I've made it onto some drug runner properties in prior missions. I don't have clothing for Montana. Do you have time to buy stuff and bring it with you?"

"You forget I can't bring luggage. It will have to fit in my pockets and backpack."

"Great, but you could put your feet in a man's size 11 snow boot, pull on man's snow pants and a parka over yours, and beam yourself here with your shoes stuffed in my jacket pockets, right, and still have room for other things in the backpack?"

"I could. I need to go shopping right now. I'm going to hang up and you can text me your sizes. See you soon."

Michelle ended the call and thought about what she was about to do. She was planning on something without her boss's knowledge or consent. They might get in the way of whatever SWAT or SEAL team the government agencies sent in. Still, she couldn't do nothing. She gathered up her coat, wallet, and phone and headed to the local sporting goods store, which that closed in less than an hour. Jason sent his sizes, as well as some suggestions for weapons other than guns. Michelle had two guns she could bring with her, but she didn't have time to buy anything for Jason. So he would get pepper spray and a knife and whatever else she came across in addition to clothing. She had so much stuff that she wasn't sure she could teleport with all of it in one go. She arrived at the airport and rented a car, which confused the rental company.

"Where did you come from? We haven't had any planes arrive for a few hours."

"I had car problems with my prior rental, and someone gave me a lift here."

"Oh, I'm sorry you had so much trouble tonight."

Michelle finished the paperwork for a car and checked her watch. Jason should be arriving at any minute. She'd go into the terminal and bring him to the car, and then she would teleport home to load herself up with the rest of the materials she thought they might need for this trip.

She spotted him and smiled like they were old friends. This was a small town, and perhaps many people knew other people. Jason had managed to change into jeans and sneakers, but the jacket he was wearing wasn't warm enough for the climate. Fortunately, she was holding the new jacket in her arms, which lent more credence to the fact that he was returning from a business trip to a warmer climate. They shared a fake hug and then turned and moved toward the exit.

"Do you have luggage?"

"No, all of my possessions are in my backpack. Thanks for getting the winter gear here."

"Yes, well, I didn't get it all here. I have to make one more trip home to get your boots and ski pants and a variety of toxic sprays. It will just take me a few moments, and the rental car lot seems deserted, so I thought I would drop you at the car with the stuff I already brought and go back for a second load."

"Okay." And they were shortly at a rental SUV that had snow tires and four-wheel drive.

She showed him what she brought, then they sat inside the car, and she disappeared for five minutes. This allowed her to put additional layers on and stuff the backpack with weapons of a sort. She popped back onto the car seat and shrugged her feet out of his boots. She showed him the weapons they had, in addition to her two guns and snow pants that he would need if he had to hike into the ranch.

"Okay, let's talk about a game plan on the way north. It will take us about ninety minutes to get there," Michelle said.

"We both felt the need to be here. You were going to try and hang out in the trees near the building. I'd like to take a surveillance area in another tree nearby. Does the property allow for that?"

"Yes, but how are you going to get close enough to find a tree for cover?"

"I have an ultra-lightweight powered paraglider in my backpack. We can park ten miles away, and I'll launch in the paraglider. I won't be as fast or as quiet as you, but I should be able to get perhaps a mile away and walk the remainder."

"Is it safe? Do you know how to fly it?"

"I've used it on other CIA missions to be inserted in or escape from a hostile zone. It will make a little noise in quiet Montana, but it was the best thing I could think of to imitate your skills. I'll be about twenty minutes behind you, but at least you'll have a backup. If it is snowing hard, then it won't work, but the snow earlier in the day seems to have stopped, so I think we're a go."

"Should we call Sheila? I worry that they have many commandoes on their way to take down this operation, and I don't want you to die out of stupidity on our part. I can always escape, but you're not mobile like me."

They argued the positives and negatives of informing Sheila as they drove the empty highway close to ten o'clock at night. They were nearing the freeway off-ramp that would take them toward the ranch. It was a large ranch of nearly one-hundred square miles, but they had a map of where the barns were in relation to the road that passed the ranch, and it was about ten miles. If Jason didn't freeze to death, it wouldn't be a long journey in the paraglider. They were at an impasse as to whether to inform Sheila Meeks.

In the late-night silence of the night, Michelle's phone rang. She debated a few rings whether to answer as it would seal their fate. She punched the button and said, "Hello."

"Hold for a moment while I get Jason on this call."

"We're together. I'll put you on speaker."

There was a brief pause, then Sheila Meeks asked, "Where are the two of you together?"

Michelle looked at Jason as if to say, *you come up with an explanation.*

He sighed and said aloud, "We're just on the boundary of the ranch in question in Montana."

"I should have figured you two would do something stupid. You didn't trust me or MacDonald or the President of the United States to get this right."

"Actually, Ma'am, it was my intent to just do surveillance until the cavalry arrived. Jason is my backup. What if they move the enriched uranium somewhere? I can follow it," Michelle said, using a more formal title with her boss as she knew they were out of line.

"True, but now I'm faced with telling my chain of command not to shoot my two operatives who are acting against my direction. Maybe I should just let you be arrested by our team," Sheila suggested with sarcasm dripping from her voice.

"Ma'am, with world destruction on the line, there's no way the two of us were going to passively sit by. We're just not made that way," Jason said. "We're coming upon where we plan to exit the car. So, we'll just sound off and text you any news."

"How are you getting to the property, Jason? We don't want

them to have advance warning that a team is about to descend on the property."

"Michelle has her way to get there, and I have an ultralight paraglider that I'll fly to about a mile away, and then I'll hike the remainder. Michelle will already be there and can warn me of any enemy activity. Please text us when we should expect your team to arrive. I assume you have a private plane landing at Malmstrom Air Force Base in about an hour or two, so your team is likely two to three hours out. A lot could happen in that time."

"Or nothing at all other than endangering the lives of two of my case officers and a secret team approved by the President," Sheila said with a sigh. "I'll call the team and have them get in touch with you. Good luck, and we'll talk about whether you two want to stay with the agency long-term. You seem to have a problem following directions."

There was dead silence, and they realized the call had ended.

"She wasn't happy with us," Michelle said.

"I wouldn't be in her position either, but I wouldn't make any changes to what we are doing tonight. I don't care if I lose my job. I, we made the right choice to come here tonight."

"Look at the bright side. It's not snowing," Michelle said. "I'm not worried about losing my job as I have too unique a skill set for them to ever let me go. Besides, I'm with you—we made the right decision. If they decide to fire you, maybe I'll use my power to have them keep you, or we could spin off and form our own agency."

"I have more to say about your ideas, but I need to get my ultralight paraglider going. I'll park under that tree, and we'll go from here. It's a straight shot back to the barn."

"Sounds like a plan, but I would recommend that you park just beyond the tree. If the branches unload their snow on the car, we might get stuck."

"Good point," Jason said, parking the car where Michelle

suggested. They went around to the back end of their rental. Jason began assembling the paraglider while Michelle followed his directions to fill the tank that would power the engine. He and Michelle put on their winter clothes and loaded their pockets with makeshift weapons. Then Michelle watched him take off, just skimming the trees toward the ranch buildings. They both were using GPS to guide them. Michelle debated pacing Jason but decided she would be more useful watching the barn for activity.

She imagined the branches of the tree near the barn and was soon making a dive to wrap her arms around the branches while she found her balance in the tree. It was some kind of oak tree, but more scraggly than the trees she was used to in California. The leaves were in the early stage of reappearing after the winter, so the branches didn't offer much concealment, but it was night-time. Once she was steady, she pulled up the app that allowed her to track Jason's progress, and he was still a few miles out but making steady progress her way.

Michelle texted Sheila about their progress. Then her eye caught a door opening at one end of the barn, and two people walked out and headed toward what she assumed was the staff living quarters. They talked, and their voices carried on the night air, but she couldn't tell what they were saying or even what language they were speaking.

Then she saw headlights coming toward the building. She texted Sheila asking if this was her team arriving.

"*No.*"

She felt like texting back: *See, it was a good thing we came out here.* But she bit her tongue.

She texted Jason with the same information: *Unfriendlies just arriving at the building. Be careful.*

He texted back: *Walking now, saw the lights, not Sheila's team?*

No.

B there in 5.

Okay. Creating group chat w/ Sheila.

Michelle took a minute to create the group and watched a heavy-duty pickup truck back up to one barn door. She wished she could see inside the barn when the door was opened, but her angle was wrong. She looked around for another oak tree to sit in but couldn't see an option. She watched as a man carried out a box that appeared heavy and placed it in the bed of the truck. She created a live video with Langley and kept her phone focused on the truck and barn entrance. She narrated the live video speaking softly.

"Heavy-duty pickup truck being loaded with what appears to be heavy boxes or otherwise square objects. One man drove up in the truck and is the only person loading."

Michelle paused and looked around to make sure that no one was approaching her. She was still safe.

"Two employees left the barn and entered employee housing perhaps no more than five minutes before the truck rolled up. I haven't seen anyone else here other than the truck driver, who is also the person loading the heavy boxes. I will take a moment to zoom in on the boxes."

Again she paused, and using her two fingers, she zoomed in on the objects being loaded. She still couldn't tell what they were.

"I'm going closer."

Michelle put the phone in her pocket then headed for the front of the truck. Fortunately, the driver had turned off his lights and shut off the engine before he started loading the cargo area. She also knew that Jason had been keeping up a brutal pace and was due to reach the truck in about another twenty strides. She watched his movement on her phone app and could see him closing in on her position. She briefly turned the light on her phone to guide him the last few steps to her.

"Welcome. The driver is loading stuff at the moment. Why don't you look around for a place to hide in case he approaches or otherwise starts the engine?" Michelle said.

Jason looked around and decided on a plan if he should need to move quickly.

"If I have a chance to get into the pickup truck bed when he leaves, I'll do so, but I also have a backup plan to hide."

"Do not get in the bed of the pickup. Who knows if that stuff is radioactive or explosive? Either way, you could die."

"True. We'd be better off if you teleported yourself every few seconds to stay behind, but not in the truck."

"Good point. I've never tried to tail a vehicle that way, but maybe I could do that. I would normally have a hard time teleporting in the dark as I need to see landmarks, and if I can't, then my imagination won't work to move me there. However, if all I needed to do was keep the truck's taillights in view, I could probably keep up. Since the roads are empty, I shouldn't get plowed down by another vehicle."

"We could also try to heave one of the containers far into the snow. Maybe the driver won't notice that one container is missing."

"Let's take a look."

They crept around the side of the truck that was away from the light coming from the barn. They listened for approaching footsteps or voices from inside. With snow on the ground, footsteps were muffled. Michelle readied the phone to slip it over the edge of the truck bed and film whatever was inside the bed. Jason, clad all in black, slowly raised his head above the truck's edge, looking for motion coming from the barn. Michelle tugged him back down.

"In my mental countdown, he should be coming out of the barn soon."

They waited and then heard a sound. Michelle peered

around the tire to make sure the guy's hands were full. If he was planning to drive away, he would come toward their side of the truck, and the gig would be up. Fortunately, his hands were full with whatever the objects were.

"Could you head to Langley and grab a radiation detector and bring it back? It would help us identify what's in the containers," Jason suggested.

"Text Sheila. My phone is being used to record this event."

Jason typed a quick text to Sheila, describing the situation, and waited for a response.

Detector on way to office. ETA less than 5mins. Will text when clear 4 pickup.

They felt the truck shift when the container was put into the bed, and then the man left to fetch another container.

He felt his phone vibrate and said, "Give me your phone. Sheila has the detector in her office."

No sooner did he feel the weight of her phone in his hand and she was gone. By the time he finished looking around, she was back at his side, digging the detector out of her pocket. He took a few seconds to admire how much her talent made the universe a better place. He edged his head up over the truck and held the detector on one of the containers. Jason brought the detector back down to look at the reading.

"No radiation," he whispered to Michelle.

"Should there be?" Michelle asked.

"I don't know, but it's safe for me to hitch a ride, and I'm going to do that."

"What if it's nothing more than uranium ore dust?"

"What if it is a nuclear bomb?"

"And it's going to bump over an uneven road in the dark? Besides the guy is stacking containers as though they contained nothing more than cartons of apple juice. Whatever is in those containers can't be very fragile or sensitive to being jostled."

"Maybe these men are stupid, but I hear what you're saying. I might be risking my life for something that has little value to this operation. However, one of us has to go. We can't let that truck leave without tracking it."

"Good idea. I have some spare trackers from our dinner and Mr. Niemi's house at home in Virginia. I'll go grab one and some duct tape. See you."

Jason thought that he would never again want to work with another partner besides Michelle. Her ability to bring things to a grave situation made all the difference in the world. Besides, she was fast on her feet in thinking of solutions. He'd been with a few partners, and all they could think of was using a gun to blast their way out of a critical situation. Michelle's teleport ability was so much better than a gun. Almost before he finished his thoughts, she was back again. He put a tracker on the truck, and they moved away to the side of the building. The lone man brought three more containers out to the truck, and then he shut the lights off in the barn and headed for the truck's driver seat. A minute later, the truck was gone, and they were surrounded by the dark, cold silence of a Montana early spring night.

SIXTEEN

"What do we do now?" Michelle asked.

"Good question. Sheila can track the truck and its contents. Her special team should descend on this property in about twenty minutes," Jason said, looking at his watch. "Let's take a quick look inside the barn."

Michelle reviewed their options and decided that Jason's suggestion was as good as anything, so she nodded, and they scrambled toward the barn.

The door was locked, and they stood staring at it blankly for a second until Michelle muttered, "Duh."

She was soon opening the door from the inside to allow Jason entry into the big building. Unfortunately, the building was in the dark, and he debated turning the lights on.

"Let's wait until the special team arrives to turn on the lights. I'd like more support than just the two of us when we don't know how many people are around the property," Michelle suggested.

"We'll shine our phones around," and they did just that.

"Oh my gosh!" Michelle exclaimed.

They were looking at rows of air tanks. Some were labeled

oxygen, while others were labeled helium or air. Michelle stared in disbelief as she had been in this room not seven hours earlier. She hadn't seen those words on the tanks.

"Did they reassemble this room earlier this evening?" Jason asked, doubtful. He hadn't been inside before, but he'd seen the video Michelle collected.

"Wait. Let me go to the other end where I filmed my video."

Using their camera flashlights, they made their way across the large room. She stopped once she was in the same spot she teleported to earlier and turned around. Again, they saw gas tanks, some with labels. Michelle switched back and forth between the video on her phone and what was in front of her.

"I think they put some kind of sleeve on the centrifuges to make them look like gas cylinders. Look at the heights of the tanks. It's the same. The same cords are coming out of the top, and the gas lines feeding the bottom of the cylinders look new. Let's see if anything has been placed on the bottom pipes that you can see in this picture."

They still had Sheila on the live feed from Michelle's phone when suddenly, the connection was ended.

"That's weird. We lost our connection to Langley. I went from four bars of reception to none. I wonder if the centrifuges or the uranium blocks cellular waves inside the building."

"Let's check the floor, and then we'll return to where we had reception," Jason said.

Using a screwdriver they noticed on a bench, they dug into the hard-packed dirt of the floor and uncovered pipes heading toward the cylinders.

"Looks like someone created a superficial cover in hopes that no one would look further. Let's take a picture and send it to Sheila. At least if we can't re-establish a connection, we might get a picture out."

They moved back to the entrance where they had phone reception, but the phone wouldn't re-connect.

"The team should be here at any time. Let's retreat to the trees to stay out of their way, and we'll try the reception outside," Jason suggested.

"Good idea," Michelle said, and they hurried outside into the cold darkness to the tree that Michelle originally perched in.

She checked her cellular reception again, and there was none. Jason's phone was also not working.

"I'll pop in and tell Sheila that there's something blocking reception here and be back quick."

He nodded and looked around his surrounding. The silence was absolute as even the wind had died down. He jumped when Michelle appeared again in front of him.

"Sheila knows our cell phones don't work here, so she handed me her personal satellite phone, so we could communicate. Let's hope this phone doesn't get blocked."

"It's hard to do. First, someone must detect the phone, then they must find the signal we use. As the team is close and likely carrying satellite communications, we should only need her sat phone for a short time. I'd recommend that we turn it on, look for messages, and turn it off to reduce the opportunity to block the phone."

Michelle nodded as she looked around the compound. While in Sheila's office, she also grabbed a set of night vision goggles and used them now to see if anyone was moving around. She didn't see movement on her first pass but then saw furtive movement on her second pass.

She passed the goggles to Jason and said, "Take a look down the road. Is that Sheila's crew or unfriendlies? I'm going to turn the sat phone on and find out."

She confirmed that the team they were waiting on was just

entering the property and so being this close to the building meant that it couldn't be their backup team.

"What should we do? I, of course, can just disappear, but I'm not going to leave you alone," Michelle said.

"You do have the best advantage in the world as a spy. Let me see if they have night vision. Maybe they can't see us."

Jason looked through the goggles, and Michelle used binoculars.

"I can't tell if they can see us," Jason said.

"Do you see weapons?"

"Yes."

"Let me get behind them and see if I can hear anything."

"Be careful."

"You too," and she was gone.

Michelle visualized an evergreen tree she could duck behind, and so she found herself peering from behind branches at the advancing group. She listened and looked at the men, assessing what they were doing. Despite the quiet of the night, their voices weren't carrying. They must be using headsets to communicate with each other. She watched their gestures and decided that they did know of Jason's whereabouts in the trees. It was time for her to cause a diversion that would occupy the unfriendlies until Sheila's team arrived.

She reached down and formed two tight snowballs and launched them at the group. As soon as they were out of her hands, she moved to the opposite side of the road and launched a few more. She continued the dance until she spotted another set of headlights on the road and knew their backup team was arriving. The team she'd been bombarding also saw the approaching headlights and immediately huddled to decide what to do. They then dispersed to either side of the road, deciding to ambush them. Michelle moved back to Jason and fired up the sat phone to warn Sheila's team of the ambush. She worried she wouldn't make the connection in time, but she did, and she noted that Sheila's team halted their approach just in the nick of time.

She and Jason moved from their location behind the tree and wove their way toward the building. There were lots of places to hide inside, and they wanted to be out of the range of fire if the two groups opened up on each other. Once inside the building, they connected to Sheila to relay their position. They heard some noise outside, but the metal building they were inside was likely lead shielded as the sound was muffled.

Eventually, Sheila asked them to open the doors for her men. Michelle and Jason went to opposite sides of the building to open the door as they weren't sure which door the team was at. Then they located light switches and put the building on full illumination.

"What is this place? A welding workshop?" asked one of the men from the special ops teams.

"That's what it is supposed to look like," Michelle replied. "But underneath it, all these are centrifuges that enrich uranium."

She then took them over and showed them what was under the dirt and how the system worked.

"Is this place radioactive or explosive?"

"No to the radiation," Jason said, holding up his radiation detector. "As to whether it is explosive, that is beyond my pay grade. I will guess this stuff is explosive if it is still here. Maybe we can figure out if there's any gas running through these pipes."

"How about the scientists in the employee bunkhouse? Perhaps they know," Michelle suggested.

That stopped everyone dead for a moment.

"I forgot all about them. Follow me," Jason said.

A couple of armed men followed Jason out of the building toward the bunkhouse, or what Michelle had thought was a bunkhouse.

"Do you have an explosives person with you? I hope no one has rigged this place to blow."

"We do, and he's been looking."

Jason returned with the men in tow and said, "The living quarters were empty. We think they might have left on electric snowmobiles. There's an empty charging station and tracks away from the bunkhouse. I've never heard of an electric snowmobile, but if it is quiet, that would explain why we didn't hear them leave."

"I think we should get out of here since we don't know if this place is rigged to blow. I recognize this equipment as uranium enrichment centrifuges, but I don't know if anything is missing," Michelle said, walking toward the exit. "We need to get the heck out of here and have nuclear experts analyze this situation."

After brief reflection and realizing that none of them understood what they were looking at in this room of centrifuges, they beat a hasty retreat outside. Part of the team had been guarding the first group of unfriendlies that Michelle and Jason observed. She was tempted to stop and question them, but she really wanted to get away from this facility.

"Can we catch a ride back with your team?" Jason asked. "We came by car and ultralight paragliders."

"Yes. We were told to take you with us. We're bringing in a few vehicles now. We also need to remove these prisoners."

Michelle and Jason stood to the side as the team did its work.

"I've enjoyed working with a partner, but it's a new experience that I have to worry about your safety instead of knowing I can just disappear when the going gets tough."

"Likewise, for me. I found myself wondering about how much ammo you had before I remembered you had a small amount, and it didn't matter as you have a special way to avoid dying and taking on the enemy."

"Aren't we a pair?" Michelle said, holding out her fist for a bump. "I wish there was another way to get off this ranch as I could quickly head home, but I'll have to wait to leave until we get back to our rental car."

"It must be hard to resist the temptation of just disappearing at whim."

"Not really. I just remember that I could die if word gets out about my special ability, and I cool my jets."

A short time later, they were dropped off at their rental car, which fortunately started immediately despite the cold. Jason was driving to the military base to catch a ride back to Virginia. Michelle departed from the passenger seat and was shortly tucked in her bed as it was just after three in the morning, and Sheila had scheduled a nine o'clock debriefing later that morning. She spared a thought for Jason, hoping he would catch some sleep on his ride home.

SEVENTEEN

Everyone looked a little sleepy-eyed the next morning. Michelle recognized some newcomers and the leader of the special ops group she had met the previous night. Jason was there and apparently made it home, as he was clean-shaven and wearing different clothes from their midnight adventure.

Sheila Meeks began the briefing with, "We have experts at the ranch in Montana, and there is evidence of enriched uranium being manufactured. There were no explosives on the building, but some of the compressed gases used in the enrichment process could have been explosive. We also tracked the truck, but it off-loaded its supplies somewhere along the way. The men that our team contained claim to know nothing about uranium. They were sent in to destroy the building. They were strictly a security force hired by some organization. We haven't found who the organization belongs to. We followed the snowmobile tracks to a road where we found two abandoned electric snowmobiles, so we'll assume the scientists got a ride on the road somewhere. We debated fingerprinting the snowmobiles, but riders would likely have gloves on given the cold."

Meeting participants tossed a few questions at Sheila about the op, and then Michelle asked, "So is this operation at an end? Has Mr. Niemi been arrested for doing something illegal like enriching uranium? Is that even illegal to do?"

"Under the nuclear non-proliferation treaty, it is illegal for him to enrich uranium. But, other than his ownership of the land, we have no connection to him. There are no records of him ever visiting the property, so we're sure that his fancy lawyers would claim he didn't visit and had no idea that someone took it over. So we're looking for evidence of his presence on the land."

"What about the truck? What might have been in those containers?" Jason asked.

"Good question. If it is enriched uranium, it would be in the form of a hockey puck. It leaves the centrifuge as a gas, then turns to a liquid, and then a solid that looks like a puck. Your containers might have contained those pucks. The containers could have been heavy as the container might have been lead-lined, which is how the pucks are transported. The container doesn't appear to contain gas as it doesn't look like it's under pressure."

"Do you know where the truck was unloaded?"

"There were two stops, according to the tracker. Each was exactly five minutes, so the off-loading could have taken place in two locations," Sheila said.

"So we have proof that someone was trying to create a nuclear bomb on a ranch in Montana. The billionaire who owns the land is rumored to be planning to blow up the world's oil fields, but we're not going to arrest him as we have no proof yet that he was aware of the activity. We have what we think are nuclear fuel pucks being transported somewhere around the US or Canada. We have a group of people under arrest who were likely on a mission to destroy the building to remove evidence of its existence. We have at least two scientists on the run somewhere," MacDonald said in summary. "What are our next steps?"

"Officer Watson, were you able to take pictures of the containers while they were loaded?" Sheila asked.

"Yes, sorry, I should have mentioned that. A lot has happened in the past twenty-four hours, and I'm minus several hours of sleep. Let me connect to your projector, and I'll put my pictures on the screen."

The group sat in silence as Michelle explained the pictures on the screen and even zoomed in to show the containers. Fortunately, they had a picture from close up when they were hiding by the side of the truck.

"At the very least, I'll notify the border and our Canadian counterparts about what may be afoot. Let's take a thirty-minute break while I do that. I feel an urgency to notify our borders."

Jason got up to get some coffee, and Michelle could see the wheels turning in his head. This was the most complicated operation she had worked on as a policewoman or a case officer for the CIA. If she was alone out in the field with her special teleport ability, what would she do next?

"Is a nuclear disk ready to blow up things, or does it have to be processed further? Do you have to have some kind of ignition to it?" Michelle asked. Nuclear weapons were way beyond her wheelhouse of understanding.

"I don't know, I'll call our subject matter expert," Sheila said, and she soon had said expert on the speaker. After the call, it was clear that more work needed to be done to the solid metal pucks. They needed fission, and that was achieved by two pucks merging into one.

"So we're looking for another piece of property, likely somewhere in North America. Let's get another list of the properties owned by Niemi, his family, and his companies and start exploring them. We should also have him under surveillance. Is there any way we could do a search of his private planes and see where he's been over the past year? You would think he would look at the locations where he wanted the production of nuclear weapons to occur given his manufacturing mindset," said Michelle.

"That's as good a suggestion as anything else," Jason agreed.

Sheila looked toward the analysts, who nodded they would carry out Michelle's suggestion. The remainder of the room's occupants listened to the key clacking of the analysts and tried to think of the next steps.

"What does a facility look like that changes these nuclear pucks into weapons? What kind of process is it?" Michelle asked.

"Let me get an expert on the line," Sheila said. "I'm going to create a fake background so that the expert can't see a room full of worried faces. Please stay quiet in the background and tap on those computer keys softly."

Soon they saw the face of a man with the Nuclear Regulatory Commission. Sheila advised him they were having a confidential conversation. She walked him through a series of questions. He recounted the story of Little Boy, the name of the bomb dropped on Hiroshima. Shortly afterward, they ended the call, and MacDonald returned.

She sighed as she sat in the chair. "That was a hard conversation. It also proved that we don't know a lot about nuclear bombs as we haven't had to contend with them in our lifetimes. The Canadians are on the lookout for those containers in the pictures. I notified our homeland security folks for the southern border as well. What happened in my absence?"

Sheila described what her team was working on and then relayed the information from the nuclear scientist.

"So our mad scientist needs to some way to fire a solid uranium piece into a hollow piece, and that creates an explosion called fission. Right?"

"Right."

"It sounds like our suspect is close to being ready. I think we should arrest him and damn the legal consequences. Pete, you and your team head to LA. We think that is where our suspect is at the moment. I would prefer that you land on the property and take him. We don't want the news media or LAPD to get in the middle of this." Pete was the team leader from last night's special op.

Pete left the room to reassemble his team.

"Michelle, I'd like you also to head west and locate our suspect. I'm sure you'll get there faster than Pete and his team," MacDonald said. "Jason, you saw the set-up at the ranch. We need someone working with our analysts to find where the product was moved to and how they plan to drop it on the oil fields. The Canadian oil field is 540,000 square miles. A single nuclear bomb is not going to take out that large an area. The trinity nuclear bomb that was used in a test didn't have a big range. Even the Hiroshima bomb only killed everything within a one-mile radius. We need to try and understand how he plans to decimate large swaths of land. Perhaps he plans to go after some central pump stations rather than destroy the entire oil field. Canada is immediately assessing the oil field to control access on the ground, but anyone could fly overhead and drop something out of a plane."

He nodded, and soon everyone was leaving the conference room, each with their own assignment. Sheila had a list of major homes of their suspect, and Jason focused on those. Too bad Michelle wasn't around to explore those. She could do it so much faster than anyone else, but she was also needed to find their suspect and sit on him until the posse arrived. She would be occupied for the next several hours, depending on where their suspect was. They still had trackers on his possessions that they had placed in his home, and Jason assumed that was why they thought he was in Southern California.

Michelle wanted to strategize with someone on where she

should teleport to track their suspect. It seemed weird to just show up on the sidewalk outside his house and wait for a car to exit. She couldn't recall seeing a helicopter pad, but why wouldn't there be one? If there was, it would be much harder to follow him. She would have to move from large building roof to roof, trying to keep the copter in sight.

"Sheila, I've never tried to tail a suspect like this one. Can you give me some advice?"

"Stay out of sight. Other than that, I don't have much to offer. Take some more tracking devices. If David Niemi heads for a plane or helicopter, I would think you could quickly place the tracking device and get out of there before anyone noticed."

"Wow, you have high expectations."

"Michelle, you might be saving the world. It's the most important job of your career with us, and your unique abilities are likely all that stand between the worldwide supply of oil and this maniac. We are eons ahead because you found the barn. Now find this guy and keep track of him until we have him in custody."

"I could really help with exploring the other properties."

"Yes, you can, and I want you back here as soon as Pete and his team have eyes on Niemi. It's going to be a long twenty-four hours."

"Okay. Can you get me a satellite phone in addition to my cellular? He may have scrambling technology like that on the property in Montana."

"Sure."

Ten minutes later, Michelle was home changing into clothes suitable for Southern California and checking her pockets and backpack for all the possible tools she might need. Fortunately, she discovered early on that she could teleport with a wig on, so she kept a few on hand when she needed to go undercover. She had a royal blue wig with goth-like make-up and black clothing.

Sometimes it was a bad idea to stand out in a crowd, but in California, it could be difficult to stand out in a crowd as fashion concepts varied so much.

She pulled out a Google map to get an idea of where she wanted to appear in Los Angeles. She needed a location near Niemi's house, but one she wasn't likely to immediately bump into people. She liked the idea of a tree as she would have a better range of views, and the majority of people wouldn't see her high in a tree. She spotted the perfect tree. It was a weeping willow with lots of foliage to partially hide her. Soon she found herself perched on the tree limb she had envisioned, making a grab for a branch for balance. She looked around and found she could look into their suspect's yard. She looked around at the other trees, looking for a better vantage point, but she didn't see one. There was a palm tree inside the compound, but she recalled that the branches were sharp, and it seemed very tall. She stayed where she was and took a quick look at her watch. Pete's team was due to arrive in five hours, so she would watch their suspect then go to work viewing more properties.

She heard car sounds below and looked to see if their suspect was in the vehicle. She looked ahead at the path it would take, and there was a red light. She teleported to the backside of the building and then walked next to the vehicle to see if she could spot the driver. A woman was driving, and so Michelle found herself back in the tree moments later. Another hour passed, and another car departed. This time she found their suspect in the back seat of the sedan. She attached a tracker to the car as she walked by. She then texted Sheila about the car and planned her next steps. She would use the app on her phone to track him. The tricky part was knowing when her suspect got out of the car. If she didn't stay close to the car, she wouldn't be able to see when he exited the car or if it was simply stopped in the flow of traffic. She followed the car on building tops looking over the edge for a glimpse of their suspect, ready to drop to street level when she needed to. Instead, their suspect's car headed for an on-ramp to one of the many freeways. Sheila could follow the car until it arrived at a destination, and then Michelle would teleport to the new location.

She leaned against the wall of the high-rise enjoying the California sun, closed her eyes, and paused for a few moments of meditation. Twenty minutes later, Sheila called with the message that he was pulling into the Santa Monica regional airport. Michelle stood up and stretched, then headed over to the airport. Sheila indicated that the car was parked outside of one of the larger hangars. She peeked around the edge of the building, spying security cameras likely scanning the area where she was standing. She looked for a better place to hide and spied some oil drums in a corner, and she was soon ducking behind them. She listened for words to give her a hint of where the plane was going but heard only quiet murmurs coming from the men preparing the plane. She took a few pictures to text to Sheila and fifteen minutes later, she watched the plane roll down the runway. It was no longer her problem. Pete would have to chase the plane down.

EIGHTEEN

After a quick wardrobe change at home, Michelle was back at headquarters with Jason looking at potential locations to explore. At the top of her list to visit was another large property–this one in Maine on an island called Frenchville. For the past one hundred years, the island's census held steady at sixty-one, but recently according to one gossip site, people were moving off the island. Again, it was a poorly populated area but was owned by a subsidiary of Niemi's company. There was heavy tree growth in the area that hid the land from satellites. Some of the trees were evergreens, while others were waiting to bloom with Spring. The island contained a private airstrip and a dock. He would want multiple ways to escape. She and Jason discussed the raw materials and work needed to convert the uranium hockey pucks into nuclear weapons. A big space wasn't necessary, and the supplies could have been delivered by ferry in a crate. The island was about nine miles long, and Michelle needed to strategize where to search. She loved the fact there were trees everywhere. If she found herself in a tight situation, she would be able to move quickly for cover.

After more conversation about where to search, Michelle said, "We seem to be going in a circle. I'm going to leave for the island now, and I'll report back what I see."

"I'll join you up there this evening after we get some more work done here," Jason said.

"Does anyone know if they found Mr. Niemi's plane?" Michelle asked.

People shook their heads, so she made a mental note to ask Sheila on her way out. It would be good to know if she was facing down their suspect or just his minions.

When she walked into the area where Sheila's assistant sat, she was glad to see the seat was empty; she would be able to teleport out of her boss's office and home to change her clothing once again before heading to Maine. She knocked on the door, having checked with Sheila that she was available to answer questions.

"Has Pete's group found the plane?"

"It's weird. The plane headed out straight over the Pacific Ocean and then disappeared from radar."

"Did it crash?"

"If it did, there are no signs of wreckage at the point where we lost signal with the plane, according to the Coast Guard."

"So you think Niemi's plane is alive and well and heading back inland over the United States?"

"I do. Knowing the guy for being a technology and manufacturing whiz, he probably has some coating on the plane that makes it hard to detect. We have FAA airport towers on alert if they spot the plane, and that's all we can do."

"Darn! I should have taken a few extra minutes to try and put a transmitter on that plane. Do you think you will find it?" Michelle asked.

"Yes, if it stays in American airspace; otherwise no."

"Okay. I'm heading over to Maine to look at a private island that he owns. It's nearly nine miles long, so I'll be awhile checking out the buildings. I'll keep the satellite phone and send you back images, hopefully. Jason will be arriving later tonight."

"How will he arrive at the island?"

"Crazy man is parachuting from an airplane to a set of coordinates I'll send him. Hopefully, this isn't a bust as he has an inflatable kayak to row to another island off the coast, and from there, he'll be picked up by a seaplane."

"I'd have thought you would have a chance to inspect the entire island before he arrives."

"I would agree with you, but we're looking for a different kind of structure than the one housing the centrifuges. It doesn't have to be large. They likely need welding equipment. Our suspect could make the outer bomb covering elsewhere and transport it to a new location to be loaded with enriched uranium. There has to be a firing mechanism inside the bomb to get the uranium explosion. I think I have that right. I've been trying to understand how bombs work and what I'm looking for."

"We have some CIA staff making drawings of what our suspect might try to make. However, we also know that our suspect has been on the cutting edge of technology for many years and may have a far better design than we think."

"Is anyone working on the question of how one destroys oil fields that are hundreds of miles in size?"

"MacDonald assures me that someone is working on that question. The information we have on the enrichment facility in Montana has been calculated to make a max of thirty to forty bombs. Suppose instead of targeting the actual oilfield, our suspect targeted key pumping stations or storage areas. In that case, he could be effective at shutting down the oil supplies for five to ten years. We would have a lot of deaths during that time from a lack of oil. There would be food shortages as crops were wasted in the fields with no transportation to market. There would be no ambulances to rush people to hospitals. If oil is used to make liquid oxygen, people will die in hospitals due to oxygen. It could be very depressing to think of all the horrible consequences if our oil supply was cut off in a flash. About ten percent of our electricity is generated by the sun, air, or water. Also, some electricity is generated by coal, but how would you get coal from the mines to power stations without oil? It really is too monstrous to think about the devastation if our suspect is successful. Instead, we need to deploy our secret weapon, which is you, to find the bomb assembly facility and stop this maniac from killing millions of people."

Michelle felt the pressure ratchet up on her ability to find the assembly facility. The CIA could send in strike teams like Pete led and stop the madness, but they had to find the madman first. What if the madman had accomplices? Given the number of people with the necessary technical skills to build a nuclear bomb, she had to think that their suspect had help.

She checked that she had everything she needed from Sheila and teleported home to change her clothing and load a backpack with things she might need if she had to spend several days on the island. The beauty of her special ability was that if she needed something at the last moment, she could go fetch it. Heck, if she wanted to sleep in her soft bed at night, she could teleport home. In this next effort at searching an island, one of the tools that Michelle had was a metal detector. Nuclear bombs were filled with metal. She also had a recent satellite picture that marked every structure on the island. The variable weather of the Maine coast required bombs to be assembled indoors.

She focused her mind on the trees near the harbor, and soon she was feeling the wind gusts coming off of the Atlantic Ocean. She looked around for other people and saw none. There should've been a lot of fishing boats in the harbor, but there were none. Perhaps they had yet to come in from a day's work of searching for fish. The scenery around her looked dismal, as though all the humans had deserted the island. She saw no businesses open and using her binoculars, Michelle could see no-trespassing signs on the harbor docks. Either there was a mass exodus of people from the island due to death or they were being paid money to leave. She checked her cellphone, and she had no reception. Time to use the satellite phone, which unfortunately was slow to transmit pictures. She looked in the distance and saw a boat that seemed to be aiming for the island. Rather than head out to explore the buildings, she paused to see if the boat was indeed docking at the island harbor.

As it got closer, she could see boxes of supplies and coolers. So she would bet that this boat contained cargo and it was supplying food for whoever was left on the island. It made sense that it would come this way as the general store had a closed sign. People needed to get their food from somewhere. She would just have to see where the food was being delivered and who was receiving it. She transmitted that intelligence back to the CIA. She almost stepped out of the trees when some movement caught the side of her eye. A silent electric car was heading toward the dock. She watched the supplies be loaded into the vehicle and noted that it would take two trips to the dock to fit all the boxes into the car. As the car drove away from the dock, Michelle skipped from tree to tree, following it to its destination. When the car arrived at a building that she could swear was not on any satellite images, she wondered if their suspect was using some cloaking technology like something out of Star Trek. She snapped more images and uploaded them to Langley. She clearly had arrived on the island just in time. Something strange was happening here that deserved to be investigated. All of the strangeness didn't mean that this is where David Niemi was building nuclear bombs, but surely this was a clue.

NINETEEN

David Niemi was bouncing a two-year-old girl on his hip while walking back and forth inside the plane. He was talking into a headset—getting a status of his various business interests. His partner and his security detail were with him on the plane. In fact, the plane had room for another fifty people. After working on his legitimate businesses, now turned his attention toward saving the planet for the girl on his hip. Sure, global warming would affect his other children, but it would have the most effect on his sweet girl.

He'd been talking with a group of scientists a couple of years ago. At the time, he'd been startled by their calculations, but it felt so far off in the future that he concluded he didn't need to worry about it. He had done his share to stop global warming with the creation of an all-electric car. Other carmakers had played catch up, but there were still far too many gas-guzzling automobiles on the roads around the world. It was time to end this. He did calculations using the same formulas the scientists used. No matter how he changed the component numbers, the earth's temperatures continued to rise along with its water level.

He'd come to the conclusion that he would have to solve global warming for his baby girl.

He spoke with an extremely small group of scientists on what would happen if he reduced the world's dependence on oil. His conversation was theoretical, he assured them, of course. He reviewed calculations with them to make sure he understood that it would work. Then he went to work on planning how to make it happen. What if he disabled all cars worldwide? All cars had chips and could be hacked into. Car and trucks were just one use of oil, but transportation as a sector accounted for about sixty-six percent of petroleum consumption. He did another calculation, and if he took all the cars off the road, it would help but not enough. Landfills, industrial uses, and livestock also played a role in CO_2 emissions.

Although fewer people would die if he just disabled cars, he really felt he needed to go further. He needed to change the world for his darling daughter, and taking away its oil for several years would do that. He also recognized that the earth would save on CO_2 emissions if there were fewer humans. Next came the question of how to accomplish destroying the oil reserves of the world. Given that the average oil well was six thousand feet deep and oil fields were hundreds of square miles, actually destroying all the fields would be nearly impossible. So instead, he planned to bomb the processing areas of the major oil fields. These were complicated pipelines that performed the functions of gas processing, refining, petrochemicals, pipelines, and transportation. Hitting just one of the areas with a bomb would cause fires for weeks or months and destroy the infrastructure necessary to move oil from in-ground to transport trucks.

He thought about this solution for a few months. In the name of saving the planet for his youngest child, he would see millions killed worldwide due to a lack of oil. Was that what he wanted? He thought that was a drastic solution. Was there some way he could hurry along the current efforts? China and the United States were the biggest CO_2 emitters. The US had lots of automobiles, while China used a lot of oil for factories and cars. His solution would shut down manufacturing in China. First because they would run out of oil, and second because they would have no transportation to move their products worldwide. The country's citizens would starve because they would be unable to import food. The world would turn into the survival of the fittest. Of course, he would have all the family members he cared about on an island compound in the middle of the Pacific Ocean. They would have food, solar-generated electricity, and everything they needed to survive the worldwide catastrophe. In five or ten years, parts of the world would be restored, but it would give mother nature a break. Once the world returned to activities that generated CO_2, the population would be greatly diminished, and the atmosphere would be restored.

He needed three weeks to put his plan in motion. First, he would shuttle the family to the island for his parents' sixtieth wedding anniversary. While they were safe on his private island, he would drop nuclear bombs on all the major oil refineries globally–Saudi Arabia, UAE, Canada, Qatar, USA, Russia, and Kuwait–via unmanned plane–about forty locations in all. There were nearly one hundred countries that produced oil, but he couldn't knock them all out. It would change the power structure to have small countries able to still sell their oil, while the biggest countries would be crippled.

He was so close to creating a brighter future for the baby girl asleep in his arms. He planned to operate the controls of the planes. He created home bases for each of the unmanned planes near the targeted countries. He'd flown over all his targets and returned the unmanned planes to base. His bombs were in the final stages of assembly, and then he would personally take them to bases around the world and load them onto the planes. He would then have the perfect symphony of unmanned planes in motion, ready to change the world for his baby girl. He was probably considered crazy at this time as he was willing to let so many lives end in pursuit of saving the earth, but David thought in time, he would be viewed as a visionary for resetting the earth's temperature at a critical time. Either the entire earth population would suffer in fifty years, or he could lower the population and reduce emissions now.

He looked down at the bundle in his arms and wondered how proud his baby girl would be when she grew up and understood how brilliant her father had been when he made the decisions he had. He visualized her doing interviews after his death about what a wonderful father he was and a visionary thinker well ahead of his time. True, he had a few scientists with him on this journey. He needed them to create the enrichment of uranium, to confirm his design of the nuclear bombs, and to build the trigger mechanism that would explode them. In total, there were five people with him on this journey. All of them were revolutionaries in the fight against planet earth warming. He'd assisted the other five with building their own compounds that they would retreat to with their families while they watched the world change without oil. As a billionaire, he'd had many properties to give people choices of where they wanted to wait out the revolution. As much as he could, he sold the remaining properties and converted the currency into gold. The coming changes would greatly devalue worldwide currencies, and he was hedging his bets. He had a vault on the family island that contain large stores of gold.

One of the five scientists was also brilliant with intelligence gathering. David Niemi knew that some government agency suspected him of doing exactly what he planned to do. He knew his idea was far-fetched, and their initial instinct would be to assume the rumor was wrong. He thought the leak of his plans had come from some of his earlier discussions with scientists. He'd been very careful when he was first exploring the topic. Still, someone must have felt his passion for the theoretical concept. He knew he had enough standing in the world at large that a public accusation of his carrying out the concept was unlikely. He thought he would have some warning, and he did. He based two of the scientists in Montana inside the uranium enrichment facility. He'd been refining uranium for almost a year and now had enough to make the necessary bombs.

His perimeter alarm at the Montana facility had been triggered. One of his scientists was sure he'd seen a woman on the property, but he said she disappeared before his very eyes. Still, after a year of no incidences, he wasn't going to take this lightly. He immediately began to move the uranium to another location. He had his scientists put a fake covering on the production facility. The covering wouldn't stand the scrutiny of experts, but he was convinced the government was stupid. Later he watched a raid on the property and knew he'd made the right choice.

He'd had to design the unmanned planes for their specific purpose. When working on the design, he threw all his prior engineering experience into making them as invisible as possible on the radar scanners. On the day he planned to bomb the refineries, if any of his unmanned planes were shot out of the sky, they would still be close enough to cause significant damage from the nuclear explosion. The bomb for Hiroshima demonstrated that impact. He added that same cloaking technology to his primary plane, knowing that he would need to move around the United States with as little visibility as possible in the final weeks leading up to his grand plan. As soon as he saw the special ops move on his facility and easily defeat his own security crew, he made arrangements to vacate Los Angeles as it would be hard to track him down.

He hadn't shared his plans with anyone in his immediate

family, including his partner. They were all soft-hearted and didn't see the world the way he did. He'd already had an excuse ready to go if he needed a quick exit, and he employed it that day. He checked the plane radar for the United States on his laptop, and the Niemi jet was staying out of sight. He was flying north between Utah and Idaho and planned to stay just south of the US/Canada border. He even planned to stop at his ranch to refuel his jet. As the ranch was large, even if the feds were at one end, his airplane fuel tank was nearly one hundred miles away, so he thought he would get in and out without being noticed. He was painting a new tail number on the plane while refueling. He was heading for a remote island off the coast of Maine, but he was landing at a Canadian airport, betting that Canadian airports were not on the lookout for him. He had a boat available that would be transporting everyone on this plane and his stockpile of enriched uranium to the island. He would send his family onto his island retreat to prepare for the anniversary party. He would be parted from his baby girl for a few weeks while he finished the final work for his grand plan to solve global warming.

The island was heavily forested and would provide great cover for his final assembly of the enriched uranium bombs. Once he finished that task, he would transport the bombs to the unmanned planes in the seven locations he would use to attack the major oil-exporting countries.

He looked up as his assistant approached with something confidential by the look on her face. Monica Torres was one of those early scientists he'd spoken with about climate change. She sensed the direction of his thoughts. She grew up in the favela of Rio de Janeiro. Teachers recognized her brilliant mind early, and she realized this was her ticket out of the favela. Eventually, she gained a Ph.D. in Atmospheric Science and became a leading researcher on climate change. She knew where David Niemi's thoughts were taking him and voiced them out loud to him first.

In the two years since, she'd become intimately involved in his plans. She'd been helping him with all aspects of his plan including sourcing scientists and locations.

He gave his baby girl back to her mother and had Monica follow him back to a conference room on the plane.

"Our security cameras show the government recognized our uranium enrichment facility. The fake coverings only confused them for a few minutes. They now have experts in there dismantling the centrifuges. They even brought dogs in to sniff for bombs. We should have thought of blowing it up," Monica said.

"How about now? Did they try and follow us?" Niemi asked with an amused smirk. He had faith in his technology to protect the plane's visibility.

"They are apparently wary of making allegations against you. So instead of calling the local police to detain you, they sent a special team from the CIA after you. You, of course, left before they got there, and they've been unable to trace this plane. There's even speculation that you crashed into the Pacific Ocean after departing."

"Is Michael monitoring their conversations?"

Michael was someone Niemi met years ago and who Niemi put on his payroll. It was always good business to know what your rivals were doing.

"Yes, to the degree that he can. He can access some of their text and email conversations, but not the verbal stuff. I'm not sure where the special operative plane is at the moment."

"Okay, keep me informed. Our friends have already arrived on the island, correct?" Niemi asked, referring to the two scientists he needed to work on the trigger mechanism that would cause the nuclear bomb explosions.

"Yes. We also have some activity on another island called Frenchville. If they look for you in Maine, they'll be on the wrong island. Ownership records show me owning this other island where my family will retreat to after we nuke the oil refineries. There's no way to trace it to you."

"Great. Hopefully, this plane will remain safe on the runway in Canada while we do our last work with the bombs. We're so close to solving climate change. I'm so happy there will be a brighter future for my daughter."

"Do you have any other orders you need to have carried out?"

He quickly ran through his plans and what needed to be done.

"Just stay on top of any conversations about what the government is up to. If I need to move my family or my plane, I'll do so."

She gave a nod and moved to return to her seat, staring at her phone.

He spent a moment looking out the window and the darkening sky. On the one hand, he felt like grinning at the thought of the new world that was coming. Yet, still, he was worried about his family until he had them all safe on the island.

He quickly became lost in his own thoughts thinking about his next steps in this plan and imaging what the world would look like when he succeeded in destroying the major oil suppliers.

TWENTY

Michelle followed the car up the road to a house and watched as a man unloaded supplies. Either there were many people on the island, or he was stocking up to get through a period of no oil. She decided to wait until he left to see if she could estimate the number of people on the island and check the building out if no one was there.

As the man walked between the house and vehicle, she studied his face. It seemed familiar, but maybe she was just tired. Between the yacht club and the special ops team, she had been around an unusually large number of people recently. He took what looked to be his last load inside and then returned to the car and headed back down the road. She watched the taillights disappear. Then she listened for sounds coming from the house but heard none. It reminded her of a large cabin-like those she saw on a TV show devoted to Maine houses. There was a shiny new aluminum roof and newly painted cedar shakes. She guessed it was about three thousand square feet. She began peering in the windows but saw no one inside. She tried the front door, and as she expected, it was unlocked. Who needed to lock their house while they ran an errand on a deserted island?

She went inside and listened, but again heard no sound. She quickly explored the house and then stepped away before the man returned with his second load. Her impression was that he was stocking up for a long time, but she hadn't a guess as to how many people would eventually live in the house. If she thought a worldwide apocalypse was coming, the last thing she would want was to live alone. Surely he had some family who would join him.

When he returned, she had her answer. There was a woman in the car. Where had she come from?

Michelle quickly teleported back to her hiding place near the harbor. She saw two boats leaving the dock and more supplies to be picked up. So the second boat brought the woman and additional supplies and luggage. She texted all this information back to Sheila on the satellite phone. She needed to work on getting a picture of the couple. If she had to, she would teleport home and send the pictures so the couple could be identified. That was the downside of satellite phones—they could be so slow to send a picture. The experts said three hours, but she had never wasted that kind of time to verify this. There was no cellular coverage on the island, and she assumed it was because there were no inhabitants, but it could also be that cellular signals were being blocked. She had to think that when there had been more inhabitants on the island, they had cellular service.

Now back at the house, she had her phone ready to snap pictures using the zoom lens. All she needed to do was catch either person walking down the front steps, and she would have a great picture. She looked at the boxes again, worried that they might contain uranium hockey pucks, but instinctively, she knew they didn't. Like all the other boxes in the house, they likely contained cans of food. That said to her that the man was stockpiling for an anticipated upcoming survivalist time. Now she just needed to snap their pictures and determine if they were doing any work assembling bombs on the island. Once she got the pictures, she'd move on to explore the other buildings. Jason would be arriving in six or seven hours, and she would need to find an excellent place for him to land. She had never parachuted out of a plane, so she wasn't sure how exactly someone could be landing. She recalled parachuters landing in stadiums on a bullseye. Was Jason that good? If he was, he could land on the road. However, the roads had heavy forests around them, and she wouldn't want him to land on the trees. She could also have him land on the beach. She texted him a question, hoping she would get the answer soon.

While her mind was thinking, her eyes were focused on the doorway. The man came out, and she took picture after picture, hoping one of them was good. She took a minute to look and was satisfied with some of the face portraits. Then, she refocused on the doorway, hoping to get the woman's portrait. Surely, she would help the man unload the vehicle. But after two more trips outside to get boxes, Michelle was convinced that the woman was unloading the boxes inside or was simply lazy and not helping the man. Apparently, the man had unloaded the vehicle completely as he now drove back to the dock.

Michelle debated how to handle getting a picture of the woman. Since she had explored the house, she knew the layout. She could teleport inside to a place where the woman wasn't likely to be, like a closet, or she could move around this forested area and try to capture her picture through the windows. She looked through the windows with her camera, but the glare coming off the glass interfered with her seeing clearly inside. She checked her watch, calculating how much time she would have before the man returned with another car load. She searched her memory for a good hiding space inside the house. She could peer through a closet door and get the picture she needed. She thought of the perfect place and was inside the house. She listened for sounds of where the woman was. She determined she was in the kitchen, and so Michelle teleported to the room next to the kitchen to get her bearings. She peered around the corner to see what the woman was up to. She was going back and forth between a box and a cabinet, putting food supplies away. Michelle saw the opportunity to take her picture and did so just as she heard the front door open. She dropped the phone into her pants pocket and was back in the forest in no time, checking the pictures on her phone. She thought they were as good as she could get without their posing. She transferred home, connected to her Wi-Fi and sent the pictures to Sheila for identification. She was back in place in under five minutes to watch the man unload the vehicle. She debated continuing to watch the couple or going to explore other buildings on the island. She found no evidence that this house would be used to assemble bombs.

She pulled up the map and began exploring houses on the island. It was really quite sad as people had lived lives in these houses but appeared to have been offered enough money to vacate the premises. She kept crossing structures off her list as she went house to house, finding none of the welding equipment that would be needed for the next phase of Niemi's operation. As darkness set in, she knew two things. First, other than the couple in the house, there wasn't a sign of human life on this island. Second, Sheila informed her that the man and woman were from Finland and were nuclear scientists. She could assume they were there to work on this horrible project, but maybe their work was already completed and this was the island they were to wait out the world disaster caused by a lack of oil. It really surprised Michelle as this wasn't a great island in her mind. It wasn't luxurious or her idea of paradise. You could survive the heat of a tropical island, but you could die in the cold of this island's winter. Yes, the forests were pretty and the ocean magnificent, but it was cold and blustery a good part of the year. Of course, if these two were from Finland, the weather probably suited them perfectly. The winters were cold, and they had that electric car, so she assumed they had some way of generating electricity beyond oil or natural gas.

It was almost a waste of time to have Jason parachute onto the island. She would have most of the buildings researched by then. They really needed a drone to make sure that there weren't any new buildings; otherwise, how would they know they searched everywhere? She called Sheila to see if Jason could bring a drone with him as most of the drones she was aware of wouldn't fit in her backpack. He might be able to bring a larger bag with him. She continued to search until it was time to meet Jason. Maybe they would stay overnight together, and she would leave him behind on the island to continue to observe. She was starting to feel like this wasn't the right place. But where had their suspect's plane gone? She knew he had more work to do. You couldn't just throw uranium pucks out of an airplane and expect something to happen.

Jason chose to try and land on the beach. On the way down, he texted her from his satellite phone, and so she shined her flashlight straight up. It was a moonless night, and he came so fast out of the dark at her she had to scramble to get out of his way. He tumbled to his knees, and she approached to help collapse and fold the parachute. She'd chosen a house for them to stay in overnight and led him there. It was warmer inside, and they could talk without worrying about being overheard by the Finnish couple if they went for a stroll along the beach. Better still, she'd discovered a six-pack of a beer brand she liked, left behind in a kitchen cabinet. She'd found a cold small creek to cool the beer. It was unlikely that the couple would be strolling through the same forest and beach as Michelle and Jason, but they couldn't take a chance on dumb bad luck, so they stayed silent until they reached the house grabbing her beer along the way.

Jason had managed to bring nice sandwiches with him that hadn't gotten crushed on his landing. Michelle supplied the water, and they discussed her findings.

"I managed to check two-thirds of the island's houses according to the map we were given. I should be able to check the rest in the morning. Then I suggest we get the drone up in the sky to make sure we didn't miss anything. If you fly and see what the drone's camera sees, I'll keep track of the couple in the cabin to make sure they don't see the drone. Then, we can explore the area around the cabin ourselves. Does that sound like a plan?"

"Yeah. It will take me some time to arrange a pickup from this island. I was going to kayak all the way to the next island, but with so little activity here, that seems like a lot of work and a waste of time. I'll have someone come pick me up half a mile offshore and take me elsewhere. If we can finish exploring this island by tomorrow evening, I'll leave then. There's a storm coming in the day after that will strand me here until the following day, so if I can make it out tomorrow afternoon or evening, I can be useful to the team much sooner."

"Have you heard anything about where our suspect is?"

"No. If we find nothing on this island, I'm not sure where we'll be sent next."

"Yes, I've been giving that a lot of thought. Why is this couple here on the island? Why did they move everyone off the island? Couldn't they just fly in welding equipment to this island to do the final work?"

"Is there a runway on the island?" Jason asked.

"Good point. I haven't discovered a runway. If they bring

welding materials, they will have to come by ferry. So maybe you'll stay here for a few more days to see if anything arrives at the dock."

"The agency would be better served to put a camera on the dock and not leave any staff behind," Jason said.

"I can't argue with that suggestion."

"So let's get some sleep and plan on an early start to finish our surveillance of this island. Did you bring a camera with you that we could stick in the trees to monitor the dock?"

"No. I'm sure if you call Sheila, she'll be able to supply you with one that you can bring back here."

Michelle nodded, and they settled down into their respective sleeping bags. The next morning they were up with the sun. Without heat, there was no way to fix a warm breakfast, so granola bars and hot coffee from a thermos had to suffice. Michelle managed to check the remaining buildings by ten. She and Jason surveyed the area around the cabin and found no manufacturing site. Michelle sat down on the ground, prepared to watch the cabin while Jason used the drone to survey the remainder of the island. He had to bring the drone back for battery changes, but after about three hours, he was done, and there were no more buildings to survey. Michelle had obtained the camera and affixed it to watch the activity on the dock and left the island. Jason took all of his belongings, and a powerboat picked him up in the late afternoon. He was soon on the continental part of Maine awaiting orders of where to go next. He received word to head back to Langley, Virginia, as there seemed no point in staying in Maine.

He was startled at the airport when he saw someone he recognized. His plans changed in a moment. Heading to a gate marked Boston was David Niemi's partner and their young child and perhaps a protective detail. He'd met her when they had dinner at Niemi's house. Jason quickly turned his back and walked in the opposite direction and behind a few people before he turned around and confirmed it was her. He took a picture and then moved away to place a call to Sheila.

Maybe their time in Maine wasn't a waste after all. Something was going on here, and he had just gotten lucky.

TWENTY-ONE

Michelle was doing her laundry after many days away from home. She gave a brief thought to whether she should stay up to date on her laundry if she was about to lose power due to David Niemi's actions. It was terrifying to think about how all of their lives would change if this madman was successful. Then, she received a call from Sheila at just after eight. It was never good news if Sheila was calling that late.

"Hello?"

"We need you. Jason just spotted Niemi's partner at the Bangor airport. She was at a commercial gate for a flight to Boston. To the best of our knowledge, she left Los Angeles with him and their child. That leads us to think he's somewhere in that region."

"That was good luck for us good guys. Is Jason on her tail through Boston?"

"No. She was apparently at the house when the two of you were at Niemi's. There's too big a risk that she would recognize him. We have someone else on the plane following her and the child. She has an infant with her—a baby less than two years old is Jason's guess. We verified her offspring's age."

"So, what's the plan? When I first looked at the map of Maine, it looked to me that there might be close to one hundred islands off the coast of that state. Of course, that's assuming he's looking at an island. There's probably just as much a chance that he's on the mainland of Maine, or perhaps across the border in Canada."

"Actually, there are forty-six hundred islands off the coast. You were a little off in your estimate. Our analysts are looking at both the owners of islands and the biggest landowners of some islands. We're not ready to go into Canada yet or involve the Canadians at all. We would hate to alarm them for no good reason. We danced around the bush with them when we called them about the uranium pucks. Once we have something to take to them, we'll dial in our colleagues."

"What do you need from me at this point? It doesn't sound like we have anything pinpointed yet. Though Maine doesn't look like a terribly large state, when you're looking for a crazed billionaire, there are many places to hide."

"Stay available and near your phone. As I said, our analysts are sorting through data, and we might end up sending you out in the middle of the night. This call is just a heads up, so I'm not trying to explain myself to you when I wake you out of a dead sleep."

"Thanks, I appreciate that. I hope you wake me out of the dead sleep because we will have a lead to follow. By the way, are there any thoughts as to how he plans to disrupt the oil reserves worldwide?"

"Yes, we discussed that, remember?"

"I believe we thought he would bomb the oil refineries close to the oil fields rather than the actual oil fields themselves. So my question is, how is he going to actually bomb those sites? Does he have a series of planes located at airports close to those oil fields?"

"Yes, we have analysts working on that question as well. It's not as simple a question as it seems. If he's using an airplane to drop bombs, then it could have a radius of say two hundred to five thousand miles from the actual drop site. He also needs to have all of those pilots on his payroll. As you can imagine, that's a huge piece of land worldwide to research. Furthermore, as a billionaire, he owns lots of lands worldwide. Some of that land is for personal use, and some of it is commercial," Sheila said.

"Like everything else in this case, it's very complicated. My prior jobs of rescuing hostages now seem so simple compared to the outcome of this case if we don't stop him in time. I'll catch some sleep after I prepare my backpack and clothing if I need to ship out in the middle of the night."

The call ended, and Michelle knew she would have trouble falling asleep given what was on the line here if they failed to stop David Niemi. She also knew that getting sleep would make her sharper at searching for their suspect. She thought about texting Jason to see what his thoughts were on where Niemi might be assembling his bombs, but she knew that even if he was awake, she would screw up her chance for any sleep that night. She tried a meditation ritual that helped her fall asleep, only to hear her phone ring around three in the morning. At least she had gotten five hours of solid sleep.

"Hello."

"David Niemi's partner is booked for first-class travel from Boston to Honolulu today. He must be planning to hide out in the Pacific somewhere while the world falls apart. We have agents following her. One of our analysts thought of searching property records by owner's occupation. It took longer than we would've liked for our software to figure out who owns the property and what their occupation is. We have another island close to the Canadian border, but it is a part of the state of Maine. I'm going to need you to go to that island as soon as possible. Jason is also making his way there. I'll leave you two to connect."

"On my way as soon as I check the weather. What's the name of the island?"

Sheila gave her the name and the coordinates and added, "Our satellite views show an empty but heavily forested island. It belongs to a woman who is an atmospheric scientist. Her name is Monica Torres, and we have no photos of her together with our suspect. However, she was one of the occupations that we're concerned with. And in fact, she is the only person with one of our targeted occupations who owns land in Maine. Given all the activity we have going on in this part of Maine, it's worth exploring her island immediately."

"Got it. I'll keep you posted with what I see once I arrive on the island."

The weather said that there would be a high of 55° with wind and rain. Fortunately, Michelle had some high-tech clothing perfect for the weather forecast. As she had loaded the backpack before she went to sleep, it didn't require much attention. She paused to think of weapons she might want to take with her. She rarely traveled with them herself, as if she got in a tight situation, she could simply disappear. She didn't need to shoot anybody. If someone else was about to pull the trigger, she could move behind them and grab the gun and drop it into her pocket and disappear or fling it out of reach. However, she gave thought to Jason, who had none of her abilities.

So, she packed a knife, pepper spray, a Taser, and a smoke bomb. She also had a few location sensors and two cameras that she could plant.

From one moment to the next, she left the warmth and comfort of her condominium for the driving rain of the Maine island perched on the Atlantic Ocean. She wondered if she'd ever get over the shock of so instantaneously changing climates. When she teleported this time, she managed to appear with her face getting the full force of the driving wind and water. She turned around with instant relief and hustled inside the forest. Although cold and damp, she was shielded from the worst of the weather. She paused to get her bearings. Her cell phone had service. Hooray. When she looked at the island from Google Earth, it appeared as though it was completely covered by forest except for rocky or sandy beaches. Before she went out exploring, she paused to text Jason.

I'm on the island. Where are you?

I'm freezing. I just swam ashore. I need to change clothes. I'm stepping inside the forest, and here are my geo-coordinates.

Be there soon.

While Michelle was amazed at what her paranormal ability allowed her to do, she occasionally gave thought to the paranormal gods and wished that her ability came with geo-coordinates instead of just landmarks when she moved around the world. She began moving around the island, searching for the position that would bring her closer to Jason. She would move up the beach and recheck her position. She arrived at his location just as he was pulling on a turtleneck shirt. She understood why he was freezing. First, he'd come ashore in a wetsuit, and then he had to change, baring his skin to the elements. Like her, Jason soon had on a high-tech jacket that quickly brought him warmth.

"Like the Brits say, filthy weather."

"Yes, this is a little different from when we dined at the yacht club in Southern California. What have you discovered so far?"

The entire conversation had taken place in the darkest of night. Michelle had only been able to see Jason because of his bare white chest while getting dressed. It was still dark, and as they were facing west, she had no idea if dawn was arriving on the horizon.

"I haven't discovered anything other than the satellite image of this island is correct. It's heavily forested in the interior, surrounded by sandy or rocky beaches on the edges. So far, I've seen no buildings and no roads, and no people. However, the only glimpse I've had on the island was traveling around trying to find you."

"Do you ever wish that your special ability could've come with GPS coordinates?"

Michelle grinned, "Funny you say that! I was just thinking that as I moved around trying to find your geo-coordinates. Don't get me wrong, I am so enormously grateful I have this life-saving skill of teleporting. However, I was just sending thoughts to the paranormal gods that when they release Michelle 2.0 teleportation skill, it should come with GPS coordinates."

She could see the white of Jason's teeth when he grinned back at her and said, "We can always think of how to improve something we have or that we use. It must be human nature. So how should we tackle exploring this island? I don't have the drone, so we'll physically have to survey it, but it's not near as large as Frenchville Island. I suggest we start walking around the edge, looking for paths into the interior of the island. If they're going to build bombs here, David Niemi needs some path beyond the shoreline. I think we should walk over to the eastern side now as it will see daylight first. It's too dark for us to see anything otherwise."

"I can't think of a better plan. Before I left, I checked out the sunrise for Bangor; it's supposed to be at 5:58, and it is four now. We should start seeing some light in the next half hour to forty-five minutes. So, let's walk on the beach, and then once it gets lighter, we can start scrambling through the trees. Should we worry about motion detectors?"

"Yes, because there were some around that building in Montana. We can use our phones for some scanning. I don't think they will have had time to hard-wire this island. I think if they have cameras or motion detectors that they'll be radiofrequency. If we use the Bluetooth function on our phones, it will tell us when it senses a Bluetooth device like a camera or motion detector. The downside of doing that is we have to keep staring at our phones. I wish we had one of those standalone detectors that would just warn us. You don't happen to have one in your condominium, do you?"

"No, I don't. Do you? I could visit your place if you have a picture and grab anything you need."

Jason thought for a moment and knew he didn't have any gadgets in his home. He usually turned in any gear that he used for an operation at the end of it. He knew that stuff went out of date quickly, so he was afraid to hold onto it for fear of the gear being obsolete.

"No, I don't have anything either. Why don't you text Sheila, and whenever she gets in the office, she can grab a detector for us. I know she's short of sleep at the moment, and I'd rather not wake her up if she's asleep."

Michelle had begun working on the text before Jason finished his thoughts. Next, they opened their phones to try and pick up radiofrequency signals, and began to walk. Finally, they reached the eastern side of the island, where they could see the light coming from the rising sun and rotating earth. She felt her phone vibrate with a text indicating that Sheila had the tool they needed and her office was clear for Michelle to come and get it.

She stopped and said to Jason, "Be back in a sec," and just like that, she disappeared before his eyes. He stayed where he was, not wanting to get into her return airspace. He didn't understand the physics of what she could do, so instead, he accepted the magic and again marveled that she had decided to use her special abilities to aid the good in this world.

Before he had too many thoughts on the subject, he startled when she returned.

She held out the device to him and said, "Sheila says hi. Have you used one before?"

"Yes."

There was enough light that they thought they could see any path that had been carved into the forest.

"I'm going to set my alarm to remind us to step inside the forest in another fifteen minutes. Our silhouettes could obviously be spotted now, but it's just a little too dark to walk inside the trees. I'm afraid I'd be tripping frequently and perhaps making crashing sounds when I hit the ground," Jason said.

She nodded, and they set off to explore the island.

"Stop!" Jason whispered and grabbed Michelle's arm to yank her back.

Michelle stepped back while Jason fiddled with the gadget. He aimed at various spots and then pointed to a path into the woods that they could just barely see in the early light. If they took that path, they would touch off the sensor.

"Is there anything else in this area? You would think they would've planted a camera."

He played around with the device and then shook his head.

"Unless the camera's hardwired, there isn't one transmitting out here. So I think we should move ahead ten to twenty feet and then parallel walk this path that we can see into the woods."

Michelle nodded her agreement and looked for a new path to take. Glad that she had waterproof hiking boots on her feet, she proceeded through the grass and into the forest. She gave thought to just teleporting inside the forest and then looking for a path, but that was a good way to likely slam her body into some branches. Sometimes good old-fashioned walking worked better.

Just as she was about to step inside the trees, she heard a click behind her, and she ducked behind a tree and looked out. After a quick glance to see if Jason was equally protected, she saw with dismay that he'd been farther behind her than she thought.

"Come out with your hands up. You're trespassing on a private island," said an accented female voice.

TWENTY-TWO

Michelle thought about briefly teleporting behind the woman and taking the gun out of her hand, but she wanted to learn more about the set-up here. So, she cooperated with the command. Jason gave her a puzzled look knowing she could have handled things differently.

"Gee whiz, lady, put the gun down. We're just a couple of kayakers out exploring the islands of Maine. There's no need for a gun, and you might have an accident with it," Michelle exclaimed.

Again there was accented English, and Michelle couldn't figure out if it was a Spanish accent or something else.

"I don't believe you're kayakers. Where is your boat? Besides, you would've had to leave the mainland in the dark. Who kayaks in the dark? You're trespassing, and I want you to leave now."

Michelle thought about grabbing inflatable kayaks off the shelves of sporting goods stores that would be closed at this hour. She could create two kayaks on the beach in less than two minutes. However, there is no way the woman in front of her wouldn't see her disappear and reappear.

"Ma'am, let us retrieve our kayaks. You can hold me at gunpoint while my friend retrieves the kayaks. She can run, and she'll be back in under ten minutes with them."

Monica Torres had watched the pair on remote camera before confronting them and knew they didn't have kayaks. However, she could delay killing both of them while she played their game for ten minutes.

"Okay, I'm setting my watch for ten minutes. Lady, you have ten minutes to retrieve your nonexistent kayaks," she said, looking at her watch, "starting now."

Michelle stepped behind a tree and moments later was looking at a selection of kayaks that she could fit in her backpack and bring back to the island. She found a foldable kayak that wouldn't fit in her backpack. She looked around for a duffel bag with straps that she could string over both shoulders that would hold the kayak. She found what she was looking for and moments later was back on the island dumping the first kayak. The second one went even faster. She had to make a third trip to grab paddles.

She heard the woman call out, "You have two minutes before I shoot the trespasser in front of me."

Michelle quickly unfolded the two kayaks, folded up the duffel bag, and stuffed it inside her backpack, throwing the paddles into the kayaks that she began dragging out of the trees.

"Here they are. We'll just start paddling toward the mainland," Michelle said as she headed toward Jason.

The woman looked confused and debated what she should do now that they had met her requirement.

Michelle rushed the two kayaks toward the water's edge, wanting to get away from the woman to keep Jason safe. She passed one kayak over to him and proceeded to get her feet wet and settled into her own kayak, rowing out into the waves. She could feel her toes as the water that had seeped into the boots was icy cold. Jason was following her lead and was rowing as well. He yelled over the surf at her, "You should've grabbed a small motor."

"I had a ten-minute limit and was trying to save your life."

"There is that," he said, and he began to paddle faster as he heard a gunshot ring out and ducked.

"That does it! Here, grab the rope of my kayak," Michelle said, throwing him the rope.

Before the woman on shore knew what happened, the gun was out of her hand and flying into the water. Jason felt the weight of Michelle's body entering the bobbing kayak, and the two of them begin paddling in earnest to a piece of land they could see in the distance.

They were soaked from water spray and rain even with the protective clothing and were frozen by the time they reached the opposite shore. Michelle was so cold she could barely think straight.

Jason's teeth were chattering as well, but he said, "We need warmth and dry clothing. Can you fetch a propane heater and a sleeping bag?"

Michelle visualized the store and wondered if she had the energy to grab that stuff from the same store? She decided she had to try. She was starting to feel sleepy from the cold. She grabbed the heater off a shelf and turned it on to make sure it worked. She loaded it in her backpack, along with a tent. She would at least get Jason inside a warm tent before she came back for a sleeping bag.

She was shocked again by how cold it was when she returned to Maine. Fortunately, the tent she grabbed was one that simply snapped open. She did so and set the heater inside. Jason was able to crawl inside. He laid sprawled on the tent bottom, eyes closed. She felt like closing her eyes too, but knew she had to go back to the store for more stuff. She slapped her face and then said, "Be right back." She got back to the store and had to hold on to a shelf to stay upright. Fortunately, the store was heated overnight. Finally, she found the energy to grab dry clothes for herself and change. She grabbed mylar blankets, sweats and shoes, and socks for him and was back inside the tent in another ten minutes.

Jason was losing warmth to the cold floor, but the tent itself was a toasty sixty degrees, she thought, thanks to the heater. He wasn't moving and looked to be asleep. She was a little warmer thanks to the dry clothes and warm store. She called Sheila to alert her of their need for rescue with their GPS coordinates, then she set about getting Jason out of his wet clothes and into dry, warm clothing. She was exhausted by the effort and soon fell asleep.

She awoke when Pete and his special operatives shook her awake to drink some warm substance.

"What time is it? Where did you come from?" Michelle asked, confused at waking from a deep sleep, then she looked over at Jason, who appeared to still be asleep. "Is he breathing?"

"Here, drink this," said a man with the word *Med* on an armored vest. "Yes, he's breathing, and his temperature has warmed up to ninety-four, but he is likely fighting hypothermia. We'll be moving him out to our vehicle. You, on the other hand, are at ninety-seven degrees, so I think with this bag of chicken noodle soup, you'll be right as rain."

The medic stepped back as two other men brought in a stretcher. They used the mylar blanket to load him onto the stretcher, and then they soon left the tent. Michelle looked outside and saw that it was perhaps mid-morning, and the rain had ended.

"OMG, the sporting goods store is probably open, and I stole this equipment from them."

The medic looked puzzled at her, so she said, "Never mind," and picked up her phone to call Sheila.

"I see that Pete's team found you both alive," Sheila said.

"They did. Thanks for the rescue. Unfortunately, I stole two foldable kayaks, four paddles, four mylar blankets, and men's and women's sweatsuits, socks and shoes, and a portable heater from the sporting goods store on Dennison Street in Tyson's Corner. Can the agency leave cash for those purchases? I wouldn't want the store owner to suspect its employees of stealing stuff in the middle of the night."

"Of course, we'll handle it. Can you get me pictures of it?"

"Yes, just a moment," and she ran after the men carrying Jason and snapped a quick couple of pictures. Then she returned to the tent to take more pictures and thought that the medic was right about the chicken noodle soup. She felt fine now.

"I just sent you pictures of what I got from the store. Does Pete's group have its orders, or should we figure out together what to do about the island?"

"I didn't understand your message earlier. You were pretty groggy from the cold, I think. Tell me again what happened."

"Jason and I met up on the island as planned. We decided we would start exploring the eastern side as it would get daylight first. Our radio frequency sensor alerted us about the same time we saw a path into the thick forest. We decided to walk a parallel path into the forest. I had just entered the forest when I heard the click of a gun being cocked--you know, that clicking sound of a semi-automatic? Jason was still out in the open. I briefly debated teleporting behind the woman and taking the weapon out of her hands, but I was curious to see what she was up to—a miscalculation on my part."

"Why do you say that?"

"I think she had cameras stashed around the island. She

laughed when we said we were kayakers. She then gave me ten minutes to come up with our kayaks."

"And you did!"

"Yes, fortunately, the sporting goods store had foldable kayaks. I grabbed a duffel bag of theirs, filled it with each kayak, and went back and forth a few times between the kayak and the paddles. Finally, I dragged the two kayaks out to the beach with two minutes to spare. She made us paddle away from the beach, which got our feet wet and frozen. We just got into the surf when she started shooting at us, and the skies opened up with rain. So I threw my kayak's rope to Jason, teleported back to the idiotic woman and took the gun out of her hands, threw it into the sea, and was back in my kayak before the next wave. That got us safely away from the island, but we were soaking wet by the time we reached the opposite shore. We dragged ourselves upon the shore, and once I got my breath back, I teleported back to the sporting goods store for dry clothes, a tent heater, and blankets. I changed into dry clothes inside the store, but I had to help Jason inside the tent change out of his wet clothing. So, his hypothermia was worse than mine. The medic said he was up to 94°, so he is out of the woods, but probably not useful today. A nice bowl of hot chicken soup fixed me up. What do you want me to do next?"

"I don't suppose you got a picture of the woman so we can identify her?"

"I didn't, but if you have a picture of the scientist who owns that island, I can probably verify whether it's her or someone else."

"I'm sending it to your cell phone now."

Michelle waited for the picture to arrive. She had cell phone reception, but it wasn't the best. Eventually, the entire file arrived, and she opened it.

"I'd say it's highly likely that the woman who pulled a gun on us is the woman in this picture. Maybe once Jason resumes consciousness, he can verify my opinion. He was standing closer to her than I was, and I have the eyes of someone in her early fifties."

"I had Pete's team arrive by car, which is what took so long for you to get help. I was afraid to send in a helicopter as it looked like the island was close enough to hear it, and I didn't want to scare off our mad scientists."

"If they are building bombs on that island, then there's at least two of them. Do we have a guess at how many people are helping David Niemi try to rid the world of oil?"

"We don't. We don't even know if they're trying to build bombs on that island. Someone shooting at you with a gun for trespassing is not unknown in many parts of America. Our analysts are doing the search of prominent scientists and their known locations around the world. I don't know if that will yield any information as this is not my area of expertise. For all I know, a graduate student can figure these things out. Frankly, I'm surprised someone else hasn't tried it before now because it sounds so simple."

"Yeah, well, they would have to be rich to start down this path. Remember the large pieces of land he has worldwide? Think of the cost of building those centrifuges and how he got the uranium ore–that took some serious cash. He's got the private jet that has some kind of cloaking technology in it. I guess the only thing that has stopped this in the past is probably that most billionaires have money invested in oil and don't want to see it destroyed."

"Don't you sound like a cynic! But I agree with you when we're done with this case, we'll suggest our fellow intelligence officers around the world should tighten the defense of their refineries, back to the question on hand now that we've solved world peace. I could have Pete and his team invade the island, or we could have you do some advance reconnaissance. As you're the only one who has been on this island, what are your thoughts?"

"Good question," Michelle had known this question would come up, and she had been quietly thinking in the background while conversing with Sheila Meeks.

There were a few moments of silence while her supervisor allowed her to weigh options.

"I stand a decent chance of being shot if I accidentally appear in front of her. Somehow, we tripped some booby-trap that she laid on the island. Maybe what I should do is appear on the island behind the tree where I had taken cover from her originally. She's not likely to be standing anywhere in that area. From there, I can follow the trail inward and see where it leads. We had cell phone service on the island, so you should be able to track my footsteps. I think there's enough junk on the forest floor that I would hear anyone trying to creep up on me. As you know, as long as I'm not unconscious, I'm able to get out of any tight situation."

"Officer Watson, I was hoping that would be your suggestion. I'd hate to send Pete's team and have someone detonate a nuclear bomb just to keep him from learning anything. I think you're the safer option-safer for you, safer for Pete's team-and the most likely to gain new intelligence. According to my phone, it's now been three hours since you originally called me to tell me about your situation. Between the time it took you to row across the passage between the island and the mainland and the time it took you to find shelter, I suspect four hours has gone by since we've last seen our suspect. Would you agree with my estimate?"

"Yes. Have you had a satellite watching the island? Has anyone left?"

"We have been watching the island and haven't seen anyone leaving."

"You would've noticed a helicopter or a boat, correct?"

"Of course." The tone of Sheila's voice said that this was a dumb question. But, hey, *cut me some slack,* she thought, *I'm still recovering from hypothermia.*

"Okay, I'll take a look and text you whatever I learn." Then she had a thought and asked Sheila, "How do I disappear in front of a team of special operatives?"

TWENTY-THREE

"Oh, good question. Let me think."

There was silence across the phone as Michelle's supervisor thought about how to keep her Case Officer safe. It was of the utmost importance that no one learned of her teleporting ability. As much as she might trust a team of special operatives, undoubtedly someone would leak what made Michelle unique.

"Pete's team has nine people, correct?"

"Yes."

"Is it possible that you could go into the woods to pee and disappear out of sight?"

Michelle looked around at the possibilities and thought she might get away with it, but it would have to be a short trip to the island. At some point, once Pete's team was deployed across the water to the island, she would have the freedom to explore without being seen. Until then, it would have to be a short scouting trip. Maybe she would start by embarrassing the men so they wouldn't pay attention to her absence. Certainly, in her years as a cop, she gave as much as she got in the ribbing department.

"I'll give it a try."

She walked over to where the men were huddled, waiting for their next orders.

"Hey, do any of you have toilet paper? The supply I brought with me got wet."

She had to silently laugh at the expressions she saw on their faces. They ranged from embarrassment to disbelief to sneers at her incompetence to ask for such an item. But, little did they know, it was to divert their attention away from her.

One of the men sighed and went through his pack, handing over a small roll.

She walked away from them, tossing over her shoulder, "I'll be a while. Thanks."

The moment she was out of sight, she teleported over to the path on the island.

She quickly looked around her to make sure that no one was around, and then she turned on the gadget that she acquired earlier to detect radiofrequency devices. She caught a faint signal that she suspected was the camera or motion detector that had caught the two of them earlier. Hopefully, it was not aimed in her direction to detect her now. She followed the path deeper into the forest with as much speed as she could muster without hitting trees. She had set her alarm before she left for the island for fifteen minutes. She figured that was all the time the men would give her before they came looking for her.

It was a fairly short trail that led to a building painted the same colors as the forest. No wonder it couldn't be seen from satellites overhead. Michelle paused and texted Sheila, sending her a picture as well. She received a reply moments later.

"Any people around?"

"Not that I can see or hear."

"Approach with caution and see if you can peer inside. Are there windows?"

"No. Probably didn't want the reflection that comes with glass."

"How many doors?"

Michelle moved quickly around the clearing containing the house but counted only one.

"One."

"Be careful, but see if you can open the door."

This was creepy, like when she was a policewoman and had to go into a dark building looking for a suspect. She slowly pushed open the door and then she smelled an all too familiar scent.

"I smell blood."

"Who's dead? Person or animal."

"Person. It's David Niemi. Gunshot wound to the heart and head. Better send in Pete's team and figure out where the female from this morning is. I'm heading back to the opposite shore."

She was soon back on the Maine mainland, walking out of the forest and toward Pete's team. They hadn't much moved from their earlier positions. As she walked toward them, Pete's phone rang, and his men tensed as they waited for orders. It was a short conversation.

"Case Officer Watson, you're to wait here while we go explore the island. It seems that we have some new intelligence to act on. I've also had a report that your partner is regaining consciousness in the heat of the vehicle that we have him stashed in."

Michelle felt like telling the arrogant operative that she was the source of his new intelligence, but concern for her personal safety was more important than her ego, so she turned on her heel and headed toward the large SUV housing Jason. The medic who had served her earlier was standing outside the running car. She could see the seats had been folded down so Jason could more or less stretch out.

"It's too hot inside for me to stay there, but he's coming around and drinking some more soup. So I'll turn the engine off soon."

Michelle nodded and said, "Thanks for your help. Your soup was magical at giving me energy, and I'm sure Jason will be on his feet soon."

She took her jacket off and then opened the car and got inside. In no time, she was sweating. Jason was sitting up working on the bowl of chicken soup.

"I understand I have you to thank for being alive."

"You're welcome. It wasn't easy, and I'm glad you survived my efforts. I went back and forth between here and the sporting goods store back home. I was able to bring a tent, thermal blankets, dry clothes and shoes for both of us, and a propane heater. After I got back the last time, it was a struggle to get your wet clothes off you and get you dressed in the dry stuff I brought. No sooner did I have you changed when I fell into an exhausted slumber next to you, which is where the medic outside found both of us. Fortunately, by then, I had warmed up to 97°, and you warmed up to ninety-four. Which sounds cold, but I looked it up, and the danger point would've been around eighty-seven degrees. We humans must be pretty tough. The chicken soup that the medic had me drink works magic. I've been back to the island to discover that our suspect is dead and the woman is missing. Now that you're conscious, perhaps you can identify her. Sheila sent us a picture of Monica Torres, the apparent owner of that island and an atmospheric scientist. You were standing closer to her and could see her features more clearly."

She held out her phone so he could take a look at the picture and confirm the identity.

"That was her, and she nearly killed us. I'm surprised that you recovered faster than I did. I have more muscle and should have handled it better."

"Yes, but I got out of the wet clothes sooner than you did. When I was in that sporting goods store, it was heated. You were out in the elements on the shore, losing body heat while I was indoors shopping. I've had a real appreciation for my special talent today."

"So Sheila sent you ahead of Pete's team to make sure it was safe for them to go over there?"

"Yes and no. We're dealing with crazy zealots who may have nuclear bombs. You don't want Pete's team rushing into that. It was better that I checked the scene out first to ensure it was safe and that someone with a trigger finger didn't accidentally set off a bomb. I have to get out of this car. It's just too hot in here. What's your temperature now?"

"I don't know, but I'm feeling warm. Send the medic in with his thermometer, and we'll see if I'm fit for duty. At the very least, he can turn the car heater off."

Michelle climbed out of the car, grateful for the bracing cold coming at her. She looked at the medic and said, "He mostly seems back to normal. Can you check his temperature and see where he's at? Then turn the heat off."

He handed her a thermometer and said, "I'm leaving with Pete. Check his temperature, and if it's over ninety-six, just take the keys out of the ignition."

"How are you getting over to the island? Surely, the team isn't kayaking."

"Of course not. The Coast Guard is on its way here from a nearby base. If you look out on the water, you can see it approaching."

"Thanks for your help and your soup. The Coast Guard is a better ride than our kayaks."

He nodded and left. Michelle supposed that if it was rumored a dead body was on the island, it would make sense that Pete would take his medic with him to confirm that condition.

She followed the medic's instructions and noted that Jason was nicely warming up. She turned the engine off and immediately felt the relief of the cooler interior.

"You should probably eat some more as hypothermia isn't easy to recover from."

"Where are we going now? There's no point in going to the island, I don't think. We need to follow Monica Torres. Did she have nuclear bombs? Where did she go with them? How did she get them off the island by herself? Or maybe David Niemi helped her load the bombs on some kind of vessel, and then she murdered him afterward. Are there any satellite pictures of her leaving the island?"

"We're awaiting orders from Sheila. I think she was waiting for you to recover. I took a picture of David Niemi's dead body. Let me pull it up."

She opened the photo and zoomed in on their suspect. She was so focused on him that she wasn't sure she paid attention to the contents of the room he was lying in. She looked out the car window and could see the Coast Guard was sending an inflatable to pick Pete's team up on the shore.

"Just a minute. I'm going to run back to the island and take a video of the room he's in."

Jason was staring at empty space a moment later, munching on an energy bar. One of Pete's team came over to the car next to the one that Jason was sitting in to retrieve something. He hoped this wasn't the moment that Michelle picked to return to the car. Then he noticed her walking toward him from the woods. She'd been trying to keep herself safe for years. He shouldn't be surprised that she took the necessary precautions around Pete's team. She said something to the other team member, but he couldn't hear through the well-insulated glass of the vehicle.

She opened the door and got in, sitting next to Jason, and began opening her phone, planning on showing him the video.

"That was wise to reappear in the forest rather than inside this vehicle. What did you tell Pete's team member?"

He was curious at the words she used to justify her disappearance and reappearance.

"When I made my first trip to the island while you were asleep, I asked to borrow a small roll of toilet paper and told them I had business to take care of in the woods that might take me a while. I set my watch to fifteen minutes and then teleported from the woods over to the island."

"That was a good excuse to use."

"It was Sheila's idea. I think my brain was still slow from the hypothermia because I hadn't thought that of that excuse myself."

"Sometime in the future, I might have to use that excuse to explain your disappearance. So I'll just have to file that away in my memory and pull it out when the time is right."

The two of them looked down at the video of the room that their suspect was lying in, and it appeared to be empty except for his body.

"Is this the only building on the island?" Jason asked. "I mean, we were looking for a small room where they could weld together steel to enclose the bomb and its firing mechanism and enriched uranium. Instead, we're staring at an empty room. I would almost wonder if she was shooting at us as trespassers except that he was our number one suspect, and now he's dead."

"I wonder how she got off the island, and I wonder how she took the uranium supply with her assuming it was on the island to start with."

"Good questions. I wonder if they have a detector to see if there ever was uranium in the room. I guess it's time to dial in Sheila to see what our next steps are."

"I agree, but all of a sudden, I feel the need to step into your forest and pee. It will be a good test of my strength. Where's my jacket?"

Michelle thought back to when the men had moved Jason out and then further back to when she wrestled him out of his clothing.

"Let me go get it. It may be too wet for you to use. I may have to find you another jacket."

She exited the car, pulling her own jacket on, and walked over to the tent. His clothing was lying on the ground. She picked up the jacket, and it was wet both inside and out. It was really amazing he hadn't died. She left it there and returned to the SUV. She looked around for Pete's group, and they were all boarding the Coast Guard vessel.

She stepped back into the car and said, "Your jacket is too wet to use. I think you're going to have to use a blanket to stay warm while you go into the woods. Or if your bladder can tolerate it, I'll teleport into your home and grab you a new jacket."

"You move so fast that I can wait for you to return with a jacket." He pulled open his phone from the backpack that she brought over to the SUV. "Here's a picture of the interior of my house. If you walk toward the front door, you'll find a coat closet. You can grab a heavy coat out of that closet and return here with it. It would be helpful if you could bring back some clean clothing."

"I need some clothing myself as well as some underwear. Like you, I had to strip everything off. I think I'll grab the duffel bag in the tent and take over wet clothing with me so I can hang it out to dry at my house. I'll then change clothes and grab a bag to bring some back for you. Be back in a flash with your jacket."

Less than two minutes later, Jason was testing his legs as he stepped outside of the SUV. Certainly, he didn't feel like he could run now, but he felt strong enough to walk to his outdoor bathroom. He returned to the SUV and asked Michelle, "While you're back in the real world, could you bring a thermos of coffee back along with more food?"

"Will do," she said, looking at the departing Coast Guard boat and relieved that there was no one to watch what she was up to. On the next trip back to their houses in Virginia, it took a little longer to brew some coffee and heat up some food in her microwave before packing it all the backpack to return to the car.

Fifteen minutes later, with his clothing changed and the food and coffee demolished, they were on the phone with Sheila.

TWENTY-FOUR

"Did you see a boat leave the island?" Michelle asked.

"Due to the heavy rain, it was impossible to get good resolution on the water or the island during that time. Pete's group is searching the island for her, but she may have flown the coop."

"Do we know how David Niemi, last seen in Southern California air space, ended up in Maine?" Jason asked.

"We don't. We haven't discovered his plane's location yet. With his death, we have more questions than answers. Other than perhaps intersecting professional interests, we don't know why these two are connected."

"When did she buy the island? What other reason is there to destroy the large oil fields of the world? Why kill Niemi if you agreed with his line of thinking in regards to climate change, and if you didn't, why not just call the police on him?" Michelle asked.

"We don't know what his delivery system was for the nuclear bombs or whom his targets were. Depending on the answers to those questions, people could achieve different outcomes," Sheila suggested.

"What kinds of outcomes?" Michelle asked. She had spent a career in criminal justice and she still hadn't figured out the brains of criminals.

"Money or power," Jason said. "The usual motives for something like this. You could collect millions in extortion or just change the balance of power by taking oil away. What would happen to a country like Saudi Arabia if you took away its oil? Its people would starve from a lack of food, and a revolution would take place. The people would become refugees as they left the kingdom searching for food."

"What do we know about her?" Michelle asked. "Where is she from? Does she have a family? Where does she work?"

"We're preparing a dossier on her. She was born in Rio de Janeiro but was educated at an American university. She's a citizen of both countries. She's published on climate change, sounding the alarm, but not anything too radical. I have no information on where she's employed or the size of her family at the moment. As for David Niemi, he would've had to fly to Maine. There's no other way to get across the country in so little time other than by jet airplane. There are some smaller municipal airports in Maine that we're researching and those across the border in Canada. We have nuclear experts on the scene in Montana and heading to Maine and Honolulu as we try to figure out why the partner flew there, if there's a connection between these two women, where the bombs were being built, and how far they got. I have to assume that Monica Torres does have the ability to finish construction on the bombs. She appears to be a lone actor at this time. We have a lot to worry about."

"Where do you need us? How can we help?" Jason asked.

"First priority is to find our new suspect, Monica Torres. Michelle, the next time you see her, know that she is armed and dangerous, and do what you can to have her in handcuffs as quickly as possible."

"Got it. Why don't I take a look at the private planes at the closest Canadian airports? Of course, I'm assuming that she's fleeing somewhere. Would she have access to Mr. Niemi's plane if he is not around? Perhaps she has another island or piece of property in this area. Can we check the Canadian real estate records? If it was a sunny and clear day, I'm fairly sure I could see Canada from where we're standing. We're that close, so it's not inconceivable."

"Boss, if you could assign a helicopter at my disposal, I might be able to keep up a little bit with my partner," Jason suggested.

"I may just do that. It will take at least an hour to get one to where you are, Jason. We need all hands on deck looking for Monica Torres. I thought David Niemi was a nut job, but so far, she seems to be a psychopathic nut job and far more dangerous to us, our country, and our future. He was at least causing world disruption out of a sense of duty to his child. Her, not so much."

"Okay, I'm off then. I'll start sending you pictures," Michelle said, waving goodbye and disappearing. Leaving silence in her wake.

"Thank God she works for us," Jason muttered, with a combination of awe and gratitude.

"Ditto. Let me work on the copter for you."

As they were ending their call, Michelle looked around the outside corner of a hangar located on a small Canadian municipal airstrip to see if anyone was watching her. There was no one about, and the doors were closed. She found herself inside and looked around for a jet and found none. All the planes inside were propeller planes that didn't have the speed of a jet. She continued to check other buildings at this airport that were tall enough to house a jet. She also took a moment to check outside and found nothing. One down four more to go—two American and two Canadian airports.

Just as she checked out the third airport, she heard a private jet roaring down the runway. She knew it was a private jet because of the sound and the fact that no commercial jets served the airport, according to their website. She stepped outside to take a picture of the departing plane and sent the picture to Sheila. The airports that she had been visiting were small, and if they had commercial service, it was one flight a day. This was the first jet engine she had heard today.

She explored the other buildings and was on to the fourth airport when she got a text from Sheila.

That last picture you sent might be the plane we were looking for. The tail number belongs to a US jet that was taken out of service a year ago. We're researching it now to see if the tail number is a fake or if the jet is back in service. Our aviation expert says it's unlikely, but that could be the correct tail number. I don't suppose you saw which way it was headed?

I didn't, but I could try following it now.

How? Never mind, my brain might blow up trying to figure it out.

Michelle smiled and returned to the airport to look for the jet. She pulled up a map on her phone and then opened Google Earth. She found a picture of a deserted road and teleported there and then looked up in the sky. She could keep this up for a while as long as she had phone reception and the plane didn't get too high. She thought it would likely be flying in its final direction once it got above ten thousand feet. So far, she was heading west with the plane, but it could still change directions and head east. If it did that, Sheila was out of luck as Michelle will be out of the land to stand on and look up in the sky for the plane. She was able to stay more or less with the plane until they reached the Montréal airspace. Then, there were too many planes in the sky, and Michelle lost it.

She called Sheila to give her the status, "Hey Sheila, I just ran out of luck. I think I'm in the airspace for the Montréal airport, and I can't tell which plane it is that I'm following. Can you do anything on your end to trace the plane that departed from Fredericksburg, New Brunswick, and headed west over Montréal?"

"I'll see what our intelligence officers can find to track the plane. I'm sure it's helpful that we have the correct tail number."

"I still have one other airport on my list. Would you like me to return to Maine and continue with the airports or go somewhere else?"

"I'll admit that I'm stumped. What would you suggest?"

"Is there anybody there in the office that could tell us how far the plane can fly before it needs fuel? Maybe that will give us a clue as to where it stopped next. What's going on back on Monica Torres' island?"

"Just a moment while I see if I can get someone to answer your first question."

Michelle saw a tree stump and went over and sat down on it. She might as well make herself comfortable. It had been a long day after not enough sleep the night before. She thought it was likely to continue this way until they stopped whoever wanted to blow up oil fields with nuclear bombs. It was just too important a topic to sleep on the job. Still, she could tell that both Sheila's and her critical thinking weren't at their best.

"Pete's team is removing the body to Dover Air Force Base, where we will collect forensics on him. We aren't ready to release the news to the world of his murder, and certainly his partner and his children have not been told. We don't have his cell phone. Perhaps Monica took it. We're pulling the records on the phone number we have for him in hopes of getting some information on how he was going to bomb the oil fields."

"Have we been able to identify any of the people on his ranch in Montana? There were a male and female who escaped on snowmobiles. Perhaps they have knowledge of what his plans were?"

"We haven't found them or any evidence of their identity, and the same with the truck that departed the ranch with the enriched uranium."

"Now that you have the tail number of his plane, and we know that it's a different number than was on the plane when it left Southern California, he had to stop somewhere to repaint it and perhaps refuel. Can someone calculate where that likely occurred? I assume he brought his partner and child east with him because he knew we were after him, and he didn't want to leave them behind to be questioned. Wherever he stopped to refuel wasn't near a commercial airport, so he brought the family east with him before sending them back west. Has the wife reached her final destination, or is she still flying somewhere?"

"Those are some excellent questions, Michelle. If I wasn't so tired, I should have thought of them myself. Let me write those down and chase some answers. At this point, why don't you return to your home and get some sleep, as I'll likely need to send you out soon? I'll bring Jason home as well, as there's no point searching by helicopter for anything in Maine."

Michelle found herself in her shower ten minutes later. It felt great to get the seawater off of her, and the heat was making her sleepy. She hadn't thought she would be able to sleep with the future of the world on the line, but she drifted off as soon as her head hit the pillow.

She was awoken from a sound sleep a few hours later.

"Michelle, I have two destinations for you. First, I need you to stop at the ranch in Montana. Not where the centrifuges are, but a different area of the property. Apparently, there's a landing strip and likely a tank for jet fuel on that property. As you know, Niemi's Montana ranch covered hundreds of miles, and we did not search all of it. I didn't even think to give instructions to search for an airstrip. The plane landed there and hasn't taken off yet. I'm sending you satellite images. The partner is on her last leg to her final destination, we believe. It's a tropical island in the Pacific. Pack two types of clothing-one for spring in Montana and the other for spring on a tropical island that will help you fit in."

"I'm going to head to Montana right away as it sounds like the plane could leave at any moment. Then I'll come back and change into tropical gear. What does that mean if Monica Torres is heading toward the island where Niemi meant to wait out the oil revolution?"

"I don't know yet."

Michelle would think about that while she changed from her pajamas into jeans, hiking boots, and a parka to deal with the weather in Montana. The overhead image that Sheila sent showed a few trees that she could teleport to for cover while she figured out what was going on. She also had a tracker in her pocket. She planned to put it in the wheel well before the plane took off again. She didn't know how the trackers worked to know if it would function at thirty-thousand feet, but it was worth a try.

Moments later, she was in a remote area of Montana looking at a private plane. No one was outside of the plane except someone in a pilot's uniform. She checked the time on her watch, and it was nearing seven at night with the sunset in the west. Good, the dim light would hide her better. A quick check of Google told her that it would take between forty-five and sixty minutes to fuel the jet. She took more pictures of the jet and then looked at the tail number to see if it had been changed again. She compared pictures and could see that it hadn't changed. She waited patiently as the pilot finished refueling, then did another walk around the plane in a final test. He boarded the jet and then retracted the steps. Michelle made the quick move to place her tracker in the wheel well and was back inside the trees before the pilot began to steer the plane toward the runway. She called Sheila.

"I texted you the number of a tracker that I found in my house and just put in the wheel well. Hopefully, it doesn't bounce off or blow out before the wheels are retracted. I don't know if you'll be able to track it, but it was worth a try. No one stepped off the plane other than the pilot. I don't know if Monica Torres is aboard. I guess I should have stepped aboard to find out just who was on the plane. The plane is continuing its westward journey, and from what I read can fly over seven thousand miles on its current fuel tank."

"Thanks. The plane that Niemi's partner is on took off from the Honolulu airport destined for the small island nation of Kiribati. In some ways, this makes sense as Kiribati is known as a country that will disappear first with rising sea waters. It's considered to be the country most affected by global warming. There are uninhabited islands in its collection of islands, so Niemi could have purchased one of them. I will say that the analysts are surprised that he picked this country as there's little healthcare, and there's a problem with freshwater, but perhaps he has technologies around these issues."

"Yes, as a billionaire, he did seem to like his conveniences. I mean, if he was truly freaked out about global warming, he wouldn't be taking a plane everywhere. Airplanes are some of the worse carbon generators."

"Yes, well, Kiribati has an embassy in Honolulu, so we've got staff working on getting some information from that country, but following his partner will likely give us the information faster. I'd like you to head to Bonriki International Airport. The plane will be landing in about an hour, and then the question is, where will she go from there? Take some water with you as they lack good water in that nation. Also, take the satellite phone with a spare battery. If anyone asks, you're with a scientific expedition. Otherwise, you'll stand out with your skin color."

"Does she have a big party with her?"

"No. I'd guess that she was traveling just with her sister and a nanny. I don't see a security team with her. The sister must have come from somewhere else as she joined her in Honolulu."

"What kind of communication do they have on the island? Do you think there was ever a plan to launch the bombs from there?"

"If you're rich enough and own a satellite, you can get communication anywhere. I don't think the plan was to launch the bombs from Kiribati as it would take too long to reach the main oil depots in the world."

"Okay, if I'm able to get the partner by herself, do you want me to question her? Do you want me to hang out at the airport to see if the other plane arrives? Is there another airport in this country I need to worry about?"

"There was a lot of activity in those islands in WWII, and the Japanese occupied some of them. While most islands have airstrips, I would not want to land on them after nearly eighty years of non-use. By the way, I've just received word that your tracker is working. Monica's plane is over Utah at the moment."

"Have you thought of the military shooting the plane down over uninhabited land in the United States?"

"We did discuss that as a strategy. However, we don't know where the bombs are, where they're supposed to be, who the targets are, and what will set off a nuclear explosion. Without answers to those questions, we need to capture Monica Torres alive. She's enough of a lunatic at this point that we don't want to confront her in the sky. I have a team on its way to Kiribati from Honolulu to act as a strike force if she lands in that country. That's the best I can do."

"Okay, then I'll pack as you suggest. After nearly dying from hypothermia yesterday, it will be nice to nearly melt in the heat."

Michelle spent a little time before her departure printing out a few maps in case she didn't have reception, even from the satellite phone, to figure out where she was going. When she was doing research on the country, she came across a curious picture of David Niemi in Kiribati to observe a total eclipse of the sun. The picture didn't say which island he was on, but perhaps one of Sheila's analysts could run it down. A moment later, the positions of the sun changed from the end of the day in Virginia to ten in the morning and blazing hot on the next calendar day.

TWENTY-FIVE

Thankfully, Michelle remembered her sunglasses. Next to having sufficient water, blocking the glare of the tropical sun was tops on her list. She teleported to an area close to the airport. It had one commercial airplane arrival and departure each day, and she had to think that those times were when there was a lot of activity in the airport. Using her binoculars, she aimed to find a better location to spy upon the incoming passengers. If Niemi's partner left the airport, Michelle would follow her. If she stayed, Michelle planned to hang out in this grove of coconut trees and watch. The brilliant part of her special ability was she could teleport home to use the bathroom or to refill her water bottles. It was an incredibly useful stakeout skill.

She texted Sheila an update of where she was and what she was looking at. If Niemi's private plane with Monica onboard was heading to this country, there was still another ten or so hours before it would arrive. It took a commercial jetliner five hours to get from California to Hawaii and another five hours from Hawaii to Kiribati. It would have to stop for fuel somewhere along the way. She couldn't imagine Niemi's partner, with a toddler, would hang around in this tiny airport for twelve hours waiting for the plane to come in. Either this was her final destination, or she had another plane lined up to take her to one of the outlying islands. There were other planes parked at the airport, but she knew she wouldn't want to climb aboard some of them and go out over the water. Of course, the partner could also take a ferry boat somewhere, she supposed, but why would there be a ferry for a private island?

While she was sitting there, she researched the country as she had both cellular and satellite reception close to the airport. This was the first country she'd been to that hadn't been mapped by Google Earth. The more she read about the country, the more she hoped both Niemi's partner and his private jet were headed to an outlying island. There were a lot of people living in tight quarters. There was no military and a small police force. Guns were outlawed. Monica Torres could do a lot of damage to many people if she arrived with enriched uranium or explosives. They were a long way away from help, and Michelle could see it coming down to a physical contest between Monica and herself.

Finally, she saw a plane coming in for a landing. It was a commercial jet and was clearly the plane she had been waiting for. She expected Niemi's partner to come out first, given her first-class seats. She was not disappointed with her analysis as the nanny stepped out first holding a toddler, followed by the woman named Kellye Arnold whom she had met at dinner at their suspect's house, as well as a second woman whom Sheila identified as a sister named Stephanie.

She took a picture and sent it to Sheila. If they got into a taxi, she would follow them into town. She noticed that Ms. Arnold spoke with someone and was directed to another part of the airport hidden by a building. Michelle looked for a place to hide while getting closer to Kellye. The nanny and sister were trailing her, as was a pile of luggage and boxes. Wherever they were going, they were taking a lot of supplies. Certainly, eyeing the infant, she would make sure she had diapers to see the infant to underpants. While she wanted to be close enough to hear, she just couldn't risk being seen.

She noticed that there were two planes waiting and wondered if both were serving Kellye and her party. Each plane had two engines and looked like it seated ten or so people. She looked across the runway and saw a control tower. If Michelle climbed on any building roof, the control tower would have a direct view of her. She had another tracking device with her, and since it appeared that everyone was outside of the plane, she decided to take a chance and leave the GPS tracker under a cabin seat. She was in and out so quickly that she didn't take the time to look around and see if there was someone on the inside of the plane. It looked too small to have an air steward, and she thought that the extra weight of another human would be discouraged in this part of the world. The Kiribati islands were thousands of miles apart, and who knew if there was a fuel source when they reached their destination.

From her place in the forest, she called Sheila to relay what she saw and her assessment of the situation. The women were leaving the main island of Kiribati and heading to a smaller one. Whatever island they picked, it had to be long enough to support a runway for these planes to land on as well as the incoming Niemi jet. She looked up the runway needs of a Gulfstream jet, and while it could land on most of the abandoned island runways, it couldn't take off. Sheila added it to her list to research. Michelle was on standby to teleport to a new island as soon as she knew where the planes were flying. She continued watching them load the planes, balancing the luggage. Perhaps forty-five minutes after the entourage began boarding, the two planes prepared for take-off. The second plane waited a long time before taking off. She thought that it was likely because there probably was only one runway where they were headed, and the first plane would have to taxi out of the way of the second plane.

The commercial jet was soon loaded with luggage and passengers, and it too left the airport, leaving just a few airport employees and silence after the recent noise. Her tracker indicated the plane was heading east, and Michelle's only thought was there was a lot of empty ocean out there. Someone on the ground here must know where the two smaller planes were headed, so when she saw a tiny office that represented the charter company whose logo was emblazoned on the side of the two planes, she decided to start there.

"Hello," she said after opening the door.

The person behind the counter looked up in surprise. Apparently, people didn't often walk into the office.

It was hot and stuffy reflecting the climate of the island and the lack of air-conditioning.

"I'd like to see more of Kiribati, and I just saw those two planes leave. Where were they going? I might book them for later this week."

"They were a special charter, and they weren't going on a tour. If you know what island you would like to visit, I can arrange a booking."

"Oh! They had so much luggage that I thought they were staying on another island."

"They are staying. Crazy Americans like yourself moving to a deserted island," he mumbled. He then added a few words in his native Gilbertese that Michelle didn't understand.

"So, Kiribati had deserted islands that you can move to? Do you buy it from the government?"

"We don't sell our land to foreigners. This charter was heading to French Polynesia."

"Oh, okay. Which Kiribati islands would I want to visit?"

Michelle let the man drone on while waiting for the moment

she could leave the hot and smelly office and head home to her condominium. Two minutes later, she was staring at her kitchen island.

She texted Sheila:

Home in Virginia. Planes on their way to French Polynesian island. Can probably get coordinates later after the staff leaves the office.

What, you didn't want to stay in paradise and wait for the man to leave?

No, the heat and smell were not my version of paradise. However, the man did say sarcastically that the French sold their islands, unlike Kiribati. So perhaps it's time to talk to the French Consulate.

There are many places to hide out in the Pacific. Thankfully your tracker is still working, and we can plot a destination in French Polynesia. The special operative team from Hawaii has been re-routed to Bora Bora. When we're ready to send you back, at least you'll have a backup.

Have you announced David Niemi's death yet?

We've contacted his parents as he wasn't married. They'll be contacting the partner and putting out a press release.

Interesting.

Yep.

It was now approaching midnight on the East Coast. Michelle would be woken in no more than three hours as the two planes would have to land by then. If her tracker failed before touchdown, she would have to go to the office in Kiribati and find where the plane was scheduled to go. Still, she needed a few hours of sleep as she hadn't gotten more than four hours during each of the last three nights. Unlike her fellow CIA case officers, she couldn't grab a nap while she traveled—that was the downside of her special talent. She went out like a light thinking about travel, and she was groaning when her cell phone began ringing.

She looked at the clock and noted that she had slept for only two hours.

"Yes?"

"Michelle, are you awake?"

"Yes," she mumbled.

"We need you in the South Pacific. We think that the planes carrying Kellye Arnold and her gang blew up about thirty minutes into the return trip to Kiribati. We need you to get on the ground and investigate."

"Okay. Do you want me to head to the island they were dropped off at, or the office where the planes departed?"

"The office and then the island."

"Okay. I just have to get dressed, and I'll go."

"Thanks, Michelle. I'm worried that we may have two crazy people on the loose with nuclear buttons. Not one. The Niemi plane appears to be headed for the same island that these two planes blew up after departing the island to return to Kiribati. We don't understand what is going on."

"Two people? Niemi's romantic partner and the atmospheric scientist? And one of them murdered the man between these two women, the father of her child. You're right. This is crazy. I'll give you a call when I know something."

Michelle changed and loaded her backpack with water, food, satellite and cellular phones, hat, and sunglasses. She found herself standing near the same forest as earlier, a quiet place to get her bearings. The airport appeared empty. She did a rough calculation and thought the planes were expected back in another two hours. Likely whatever workers were necessary for the two planes would come back to the airport just before they were needed. Somehow they would receive notice that the two planes were not returning. Knowing Sheila, she had satellites trained on the two planes and would have caught the explosion from space. The door to the office she had stood in earlier was closed, and Michelle could see no movement inside. She teleported inside the building and did her usual full turn around the room to make sure no one was watching and to search for cameras. She found neither human nor camera watching her. She walked behind the desk and looked for the paperwork for the flights that had been chartered. She snapped pictures of what she saw and sent them to Sheila with the comment that the words must be in Gilbertese as she didn't understand them. The destination on the paperwork was Sativa Atoll which was uninhabited. So how did they get from Sativa to somewhere else? There was about a three-hundred-mile difference. That wasn't an accident. Something strange had happened in the middle of the ocean. She copied it all and sent it to Sheila.

Then she brought up some pictures and teleported to Sativa Atoll. She moved around the island and found not a soul there. It was just her, coconut trees, sea breeze, and lapping waves. Next, she visited a runway that looked like it hadn't been used since WWII. There were no tire tracks, smashed weeds, or air-disbursed sand on the runway. She sent more pictures to Sheila, then headed toward the next island that Ms. Arnold and the party had actually visited. She had a small smile as she moved from island to island. She remembered how she had wanted to take a quick sun-drenched vacation in the Caribbean after her time in Siberia at the beginning of this case. After chasing their suspects first through cold Montana and Maine and now through various tropical islands, she decided the best place she had visited in the past month was her own tiny ranch in San Martin, California.

These Pacific Ocean islands were usually skinny and circular, with coral reefs around them and lagoons in the center. The water looked beautiful, and the sand was unspoiled. For a woman with Michelle's special skills, she could search the island quickly and determine whether or not it contained humans. There must have been a boat or a plane that took them somewhere else. She had a faint thought for the toddler who had traveled so much in the past twenty-four hours. She hoped the baby didn't get sick from all the climate changes she experienced in that short time in each location. Given the load of luggage Michelle had seen at the Kiribati airport, she thought of a boat as the more likely option. Hopefully, Sheila had the US spy satellites trained on this part of the world. She had no idea where to head next. Maybe she should just find some shade and take a nap, but there was something creepy about being all by yourself in the middle of nowhere. Who would have thought? It was time to go back home. She texted Sheila that she was heading home, and a moment later, she was in her bed and cold from the cooler temperature. She lay down and pulled up the comforter and waited to find out where to go next.

Michelle got another hour of sleep before she got another call.

"Apparently, after they and their luggage were dropped off and the two planes left for their return trip to Kiribati, a floatplane arrived and carted them and their possessions off the island."

"So, where is the plane now?"

"We don't know yet. It has a range of about 750 miles roundtrip, so somewhere within probably about three-hundred miles."

"How many islands in that radius of three-hundred? Are we looking strictly at uninhabited islands?"

"I don't know. Initially, I thought yes, but there are many sparsely inhabited islands that would make great hiding places."

"Are there any islands with new installations of solar panels or wind turbines?"

"Unfortunately for our purposes, yes, there are several. However, that factor will help us narrow it down."

"Can a floatplane land anywhere? Like water or sand or land? If it lands in the water, do you need a dock to park it at?"

"All good questions. Let me get those answered, then we may have limited our search area."

"Okay, where is Niemi's jet?" Michelle asked. She wondered how the two women were going to connect and what they would say to each other when they came face to face. Something like, "Hey, I killed your partner quickly, so he felt no pain?"

She tuned back into Sheila, who said, "The plane landed on one of the smaller islands after dark. It said it was having mechanical problems. The pilot landed the plane, and then Ms. Torres ran out the door and disappeared before authorities boarded the jet. Unfortunately, the airport personnel weren't getting a response from the pilots, and it was locked from the outside. Eventually, they were able to break in, and the stench was bad as it was hot inside, and both pilots were dead. As you can imagine, French Polynesia has joined the United States in looking for this person."

"Did the floatplane approach this island?"

"We don't know. We don't have eyes on one hundred percent of the world at all times. As this is a low-key area of the world, it's taken some hustling to get information from high above. We are reorienting our spy satellites, but the ocean is big, and it's an unremitting blue except for the odd coral island. It's not an easy search. Imagine searching for something the size of a large SUV in the continental United States—the resolution required to see it means that there would be a lot of zooming in and then discovering that it wasn't what you were looking for. That's how this search is going. Just think if someone is out on the ocean fishing from one of these many islands. Then picture how long it takes an analyst to figure out who is on the boat."

"Yikes. So besides the floatplane, we have to worry about this woman escaping by boat. What island am I heading to? What language do they speak? I'll look up the weather and time myself. Do you have a US rep in Tahiti?"

"Yes, but she'll be of no help to you. We'll have to send in resources to handle this problem. Based on the fact that Torres left the plane carrying a small duffle bag that didn't look heavy by the way she was carrying it, we don't think she has the uranium disks with her."

"I would have said that we don't even know if these women are planning a nuclear attack except that between the two of them, they've killed at least five people. Jason and I could have been their sixth and seventh."

"Yes. Head out to Maurito Island. It's where the plane landed. Take handcuffs and pepper spray so you can take the woman into custody if you find her. Call me if you can't find her. The team I had waiting in Bora Bora is on its way and should land within the hour for backup. I'd rather keep this away from the French authorities, but they'll see an American military team land and know something is going on. Of course, someone else is working with the French. That's not my concern."

"Okay. I'll keep you posted."

Michelle packed her stuff, including the items that Sheila mentioned. She checked the time; it would be dark on the island for another three hours. So she grabbed her night-vision goggles, checked the weather, grabbed a map and a picture of the island, and she was off to another island in paradise.

TWENTY-SIX

Immediately, she could tell the difference between these two island groups. French Polynesia was cooler and smelled better. There were mountains on many islands, which helped with rain, agriculture, and climate change. They weren't so worried about the ocean covering their country with water. She would have to add these islands to her list of travel destinations. She could see herself getting to the island with just her backpack and teleportation. No need to suffer through a long airplane ride when all she needed was a bathing suit and a few sundresses. She must be sleep-deprived to be thinking about apparel instead of the peril she faced.

She knew this island had six thousand inhabitants and twice as many tourists, which left many places for Monica Torres to hide. Of course, that was assuming she was still on the island. Maybe she had already left on a floatplane or boat. However, Michelle would personally search the island just to make sure. She started at the airport. She saw the sad corporate jet with spotlights on it and people working the scene. She looked at the runway and realized their suspect had stopped the plane in the middle of it, which would block other planes from landing and take-off. Someone was using a tractor to try and tow the plane off the active runway. Until that happened, the locals would have to contend with the situation, and Sheila's backup team wouldn't be landing.

She looked away from the lit plane and into the beginning of the foliage near the airport and began her search. It had been between two and three hours since the woman had hopped out of the plane. She could have reached just about any point on the island. She could also steal a boat and head out into the ocean and wait for the floatplane to pick her up, but personally, Michelle thought someone probably would be nuts to do that. But, of course, this woman was insane on some level between the murders she committed and potentially her desire to blow up the world's oil fields.

The more Michelle thought about it, the more she was convinced that the woman would charter or steal a boat to get out onto the ocean and meet that floatplane. Looking for a boat bobbing in the ocean via satellite would be very difficult. Like most islands of French Polynesia, the island she was on was circular with the reef and a lagoon. If she was going to steal a boat, it would have to be larger than a single-occupant fishing boat. Especially as she felt the wind picking up. Higher wind usually meant higher waves, and the last thing you wanted when you're out in a boat is high waves. Michelle studied her map and traveled to the largest dock area. There were small boats tied up around the coast of this island, but their suspect would have to go farther out than was comfortable in a small boat to meet the plane without being seen. She also needed a lot of gas. Flying the float-plane took fuel, but maybe wherever Kellye Arnold was hiding out had its own fuel tank. That was, of course, assuming the two women were planning to meet up. She couldn't think of any other reason for both of them to be in the same hemisphere.

She was about to put her night-vision goggles on when she felt an incoming text.

Mr. Niemi's father knows where the island is located and gave us the coordinates. Apparently, the entire family was supposed to fly there this week to celebrate a family event. It is the parents sixtieth wedding anniversary. Instead, they're staying home and burying a son.

It's dark here—three in the morning. I'm using night-vision goggles to see if Monica is stealing a boat from the only large boat marina on this island. Do you want me to stay or go to the other island?

Monica seems more dangerous and knowledgeable than Kellye. Stay on your search for her. I have another team working on the island that we suspect Kellye is on.

Okay. The weather seems to be changing in my favor. The wind has picked up, and the waves are crashing harder. That should make it harder to pilot a boat or plane out in the Pacific. The radar shows this will last for about twelve hours which will hopefully keep her on the island. But, of course, that's if she hasn't already left. If she dies out in rough seas, we'll never know.

Good luck.

The day seemed a little more hopeful. At least they knew the location of the island that might be the command center for setting off devastating nuclear bombs. Michelle resettled her night-vision goggles and studied the area around this port. Fortunately, it wasn't large, and judging by the size of the boats at the marina, these were visiting yacht owners. She could read a few of the boats' home cities. She wondered if the boats were empty— were their owners taking the opportunity to stay ashore at a hotel? The marina was completely dark from what she could see. She decided to stay where she was and study the area. She thought of a question to ask Sheila and sent her a text.

Can you check with the father and see if there's an ocean-going boat docked at their private island?

She continued to scan the marina while waiting for an answer. She saw something flashing on the horizon and realized in time that it was a boat coming into the harbor. Then she heard a sound behind her like there were branches rustling. It took a moment for her to recognize the sound of movement rather than the wind. On impulse, she decided to move, and it was a good thing she did, as she heard the unmistakable sound of suppressed gunfire. She didn't know if the aim would have been true, but she was glad she followed her instinct and moved rather than turning around. She moved to another part of the area near the marina and refocused her glasses on where she'd been standing. Monica Torres now occupied that spot and was using the gun to push aside bushes looking for her. Michelle spared a glance at the marina and spotted one boat with a light on that hadn't been lit before. Had someone heard the gunshot? She also looked out on the water and saw the other boat getting closer. It still didn't have its exterior lights on and must be approaching the harbor by radar. The boat light that had turned on inside one of the marina's boats turned back off. Was that a signal?

She turned back to look at the line of foliage that she was hiding behind and saw that her suspect was still searching for her. Sheila Meeks said to take their suspect into custody. She'd best do so now while the boat was still out in the harbor. Michelle planned to use everything at her disposal to wrestle the woman to the ground. She dug out her pepper spray, gloves, zip ties, goggles, and a taped-up washcloth. She then quickly moved behind the woman and had her immobilized, her mouth stuffed with the washcloth. Monica struggled with the pepper spray pain in her eyes. Michele would have felt bad, but the woman tried to murder her less than five minutes ago. She deserved no sympathy.

In no time, Michelle had Monica quietly subdued in the bushes. She dialed Sheila.

"I have Monica Torres in custody. It's dark and four in the morning. What should I do with her? I guess I should've asked that question from the start. Also, I may have an unfriendly arriving. There's a boat coming into the marina with no lighting."

"Good job, Michelle. That boat should be your backup. They should be able to help you remove Monica from that island. I'm going to connect you now."

Monica heard a lot of wind noise and then a female voice.

"Ma'am, this is Lieutenant Nicole Chapman. We have your island in sight and should be there in the harbor in ten minutes."

"Ten minutes?" Michelle asked, watching the boat nearing the dock of the marina.

"Yes, that is what our navigational gear says."

"We may have a problem as there is another boat docking at the marina right now. It's acting covertly and not like a nighttime fisherman worried about securing his catch. So perhaps you can speed it up, as I can't drag our suspect anywhere."

"I'll do what I can, Ma'am. What's your position?"

Michelle gave her the coordinates and ended the call as she didn't want the distraction of the phone. She decided to step away from Monica as she was secured and somewhat hidden in the bushes. She would watch the new boat's occupants to see if they were looking for Monica. If necessary, she would truss them up too.

The boat was tied down at the marina. It was a decent-sized boat—bigger than the one featured on Gilligan's Island and perhaps the length of the jungle cruise boat at Disneyland. Now she could see two people—a man and a woman. The woman stayed behind with the boat while the man hopped off and started heading toward where Monica was face down. She should be hidden by the bushes. He called her name as he got closer, though it was really a large whisper.

Michelle looked out beyond the marina for her backup boat to arrive. She texted Sheila her status and a picture of the unfriendly boat that the incoming boat should block and seize. The man was nearly on top of Monica, and as Michelle watched, he froze and looked down. Darn, she was going to have to take him out. On the bright side, she supposed that the more people they had in custody, the fewer fingers there were to push the nuclear trigger.

She watched for the perfect moment and did the same thing to the man that she had to Monica. While he was contending with pepper spray, she had his hands tied behind his back, and then his mouth was stuffed and taped in place before he knew what hit him. He made a little noise on his way to the ground, and the woman over on the boat had stared in their direction, but the dark was too penetrating for her to see. The woman watched the area where Michelle stood, but she must have heard the other boat coming out of the dark toward her and decided to desert her compatriots.

Sure enough, she heard a boat starting in the distance and being put in a low motor speed to move away from the dock. The woman was caught in a hugely bright spotlight and had nowhere to go. Michelle was pleased that the Lieutenant was trying to keep her operation quiet. There was no loud sound over a public address speaker, and the light was turned off as soon as it could be. She watched as someone jumped from Lieutenant Chapman's boat and into the other boat, taking the woman into custody and placing zip ties on her wrist before she was escorted off the boat and someone else tied it up at the dock.

Michelle turned on the flashlight function of her cell phone to signal to the Lieutenant where she was located. In a short time, a group of men in military fatigues approached her. She pointed to her two captives and then walked over to the Lieutenant to thank her for her help. While she was walking, she tried to think of an excuse not to leave this island with the Lieutenant's crew. In the end, she decided to lie.

"I'm going to stay behind on this island as I've been asked to take a look at the plane."

"Ma'am, are you sure? We can get you off the island sooner than the next plane or ferry to arrive here."

"Yes. This is a small island, and my handlers are worried that the local police will screw up the evidence collection that will be necessary to bring these three to trial back in the United States," Michelle said, and she silently patted herself on the back for such a good last-moment excuse. Somehow, she didn't think the Lieutenant would believe her if she said that with her teleportation skill, she was far faster than anything that the US military owned and operated. So, she just smiled and waved goodbye. The moment she was out of sight, she called Sheila to give her an update and get a picture of the private island where Kellye Arnold was up to no good.

"Lieutenant Chapman has your three prisoners on her boat. So it's three down, four if I count David Niemi, with one more bad person out there for me to capture. That's assuming Niemi's partner's nanny and sister are not a part of this horrible idea of blowing up the world's oil refineries."

"Good work, Michelle! We dispatched a ship from Honolulu two days ago, figuring we might need some help somewhere around the middle of the Pacific Ocean. It's a special new military ship with speeds of sixty miles per hour, and so it could reach French Polynesia in less than two days. We weren't wrong in that judgment. We should have some folks that excel at interrogation aboard the bigger boat where the Lieutenant is taking those prisoners."

Michelle could hear the smirk in her boss's voice. She must

be feeling good to have so many of the criminals in custody. So true, but . . . they still had no idea how this group planned to destroy the oil fields. Were all five criminals equal in this venture? Could Kellye Arnold set off the nuclear bombs? Were they any better off than they were a month ago when she began her search for the truth regarding the rumors? There was silence on the other end of the phone, and she realized that Sheila had asked her a question that she hadn't answered.

"Whoops, I was thinking about this entire lot of criminals. What was your question?"

"Michelle, you're entitled to drift off. If not for you and your special abilities, we would be sailing off into Armageddon. I wish the entire country could thank you, but that's not the way the CIA works, nor is that good for your personal safety."

"Sheila, you know I don't need or want public recognition. I'm so satisfied with capturing Monica Torres that I'll feel good about it the remainder of the day. My problem is I haven't had coffee, and I've been bouncing between time zones so much that my body doesn't know whether to crave sleep or a hamburger."

"I can only faintly imagine what it's like for all the time travel you've done in the past week, let alone weather. Back to business, so listen to me. I'm sending you to the private island that Kellye Arnold is supposed to be on. I want you to capture her and any co-conspirators on the island. The team we dispatched to Bora Bora is now sitting on the same military boat as Lieutenant Chapman is heading to. They have a helicopter aboard that can move them faster than the ship. They are heading toward the island that was David Niemi's and will be there in about three hours. Depending on what you find, the helicopter can take off with a team and arrive sooner. I'm sending you a daytime satellite photo of the island with the coordinates. Call me as soon as you have information."

"Will do."

Michelle sat on a log, waiting for the necessary pictures to come through. As soon as she had them and after a quick pit stop in her bathroom in her condominium back in Virginia, she arrived on a new island. It was a private island. It was smaller than both the Kiribati and French Polynesian islands she had visited so far. There was a house, a dock, and extensive solar panels, and some other buildings. She couldn't find a single human on this island. It was still dark though it was starting to lighten just the tiniest bit. People should be asleep in their beds. Instead, no one seemed to be on the island. She dialed Sheila.

"This island is uninhabited at the moment. There's a house and some other building, but no one is around or asleep in any bed that I can find. Has the father been to this island before? Maybe he gave us the wrong coordinates."

"I'll check."

Michelle waited in silence, then her phone rang.

"No, he is sure he gave us the right coordinates, and he described the island as you have, and the picture I sent you also was approved by him. But, damn, where is Kellye Arnold?"

"I don't know. Shouldn't the two suspects from the boat know the location of where she's hiding? Could someone look at the gas tanks on the boat and calculate the maximum distance it could travel? I'm going to head home as it is creepy to be on deserted islands in the dark. Call me when you want me to go somewhere."

"Darn, we left the boat behind at the dock. It seemed at the time far more important to take our three prisoners back to our boat and question them. Do me a big favor and find the name and tags for the boat as well as the fuel in it."

"Okay, but I may need some help with measuring gas. I've never done that before."

"We'll have people here to walk you through it if need be.

Some tanks have an external gauge, and you might just have to look at it."

"Great! Let me end this conversation and go take some pictures."

In the future, when she wasn't on an operation, she would have to test with Sheila whether she could travel with a live cellular connection. If she had a headset on and the phone in her pocket, it would physically make it, but she assumed the call would be dropped as it would not find a cellular tower to communicate with while she teleported.

She moved to the dock and took pictures of the boat. The lights were still off in the pleasure boats tied in their moorings. She stepped onto the boat, looking for the fuel tanks. There were outboard motors at the rear, which meant that gas tanks had to be close by. As Sheila had hoped, there were meters on the gas tanks that indicated their fill levels, and the outside listed the size of the container in liters. Michelle snapped pictures and then searched the boat for additional fuel containers. She found one more fuel container. After snapping pictures of every conceivable thing on the boat, she forwarded the pictures back to Virginia and then headed there herself. She thought about taking fingerprints, but the boat looked to be a rental and would therefore have lots of fingerprints on it. Besides, their suspects were in custody, and they could fingerprint the real fingers.

She was soon resting under her comforter, waiting for the next call to come.

TWENTY-SEVEN

Kellye Arnold was frustrated. The boat that was supposed to pick up Monica Torres should have returned by now, and she was not answering her cell phone. That meant either she had been captured by the authorities, or they had drowned out on the open ocean with the higher winds and waves. She would give her another hour to show up, and then she would take matters into her own hands. When she discovered her partner, David Niemi's, plan for the world, she developed her own plan. She'd had his baby, but he didn't think she was good enough to marry. David and Monica wanted to save the world from climate change. David at least had been pure in thought, thinking his actions would make the world a better place for their daughter.

Monica wanted to save the world from climate change and topple the dictators of South America who had oil but didn't use it to make their citizens' lives better. She was going to wipe out the world's major oil supplies and take control of what was left and sell it to give the money back to her people living in the slums of Rio de Janeiro.

Kellye thought that was all crap. Forget climate change and forget controlling oil. Her ambitions were far bigger.

She wanted to be Empress of the World.

She tried to think of a fitting title for her future occupation Queen of Earth, Goddess of Earth, Protector of the Planet. She finally settled on World Empress as it was a grand name and an appropriate title for what she planned to be.

She had a little demo planned. Fortunately, her partner had shared his plans with her so she could carry them out with a few minor changes. She needed Monica and the crew in Montana to put the finishing touches on the bombs as she didn't understand how to do that. Then she had a truck drive away with the bombs, and she arranged for them to be loaded on the unmanned planes. Monica had helped with that and had killed David on her behalf. However, Kellye knew the locations and knew how to steer the unmanned airplanes. She was going to launch her first attack and threaten the world in another hour. Either Monica would be back to enjoy the experience with her, or she was gone forever.

Her husband planned to destroy the world's largest oil fields to save the planet. Why just do that when you could do more and be rich and powerful afterward? He didn't think that way as he was already rich and powerful. She was going to target the oil refinery in Equatorial Guinea. They weren't large producers of oil, but it would be a solid demonstration of her skills, and maybe she would do enough damage to knock the horrible dictator of that country out of office. It would be a win-win for that country's citizens. David had an unmanned plane parked in a small cove of a man-made lake in Egypt. He had planned to use the plane to drop a nuclear bomb on two of the Saudi refineries. Instead, she was going to demonstrate her power on Malabo, on the island of Bioka, where the small African country stored its oil reserves. Once the world saw what she could accomplish, they would meet her needs or be destroyed. She was looking forward to the fear she could create around the world. She already had her message translated into several languages, ready to go.

Each major oil-producing country would be required to sign a document stating that she was the Empress of the World and wire to a bank account in the Caribbean a one-hundred-million-dollar retainer fee. As far as she was concerned, it was the return of the Amazonian women. One day her daughter would be the second ruler of the world. She hadn't decided where she wanted to command the planet from, but Los Angeles might be the new capital of Earth. Maybe she would build a palace in Malibu as it had the most perfect weather. But, first, she needed to demonstrate her power.

Her boyfriend had built a gaming room mostly for his older children. In fact, this was his ex-wife's home. He showed her how he flew the unmanned aircraft on his laptop. She practiced when he wasn't around and pretended that understanding his dream was beyond her brain. She told him she wasn't a scientist or an economist, and he let it go. He underestimated her many times during their relationship, and for that, he paid with his life. Still, he was so enamored with their daughter, he'd likely be pleased that she would be a future Empress of the World. His final gift to her and their daughter was explaining how to load the unmanned planes with his homemade nuclear bombs. He even showed her how to fill the cabin of the tiny aircraft with C_4, which would detonate the enriched uranium. She only hoped the planes worked.

Kellye checked her watch again, and she was down to her self-appointed time to fly her plane in just thirty minutes. It would be dark in Africa, which would give cover to the unmanned plane. This was the first major step of her plan, and she was so excited to see what would happen. She spent the next thirty minutes sipping some red wine and randomly viewing cameras around the island to look for activity. Well, time was up.

It was time to take that first step as Empress of the World. She checked for perhaps the tenth time what the coordinates were for the oil refinery that was her target in Equatorial Guinea. She verified that the plane's navigation system would take it there. She maneuvered the plane remotely to a runway of sorts, and soon it was airborne. It would take a little more than three hours to arrive at the target. In the interim, she was steering it across some very boring land. She knew there were endless piles of sand below the plane.

She heard the door open behind her and looked to see her sister come into the room.

"So, are you Empress of the World yet?"

"I'm on my way. I'm flying over the Sahara Desert on my way to blow up the oil reserves of Equatorial Guinea. I think that will get the world's attention. I'm sure the politicians know that they can't deny their citizens oil. There would be an uprising that the world hasn't seen for almost one hundred years. They're going to have forty-eight hours to sign my document crowning me Empress of the World. Also, they have another twenty-four hours to transfer a hundred million dollars to a numbered bank account in the Caribbean."

"Are you sure you want to do this? You know the full force of the United States will be after you, let alone the other countries of the world. Your daughter will not be safe. Just checking in with you that you are ready to withstand the heat of the coming week."

"Are you doubting me, Stephanie?"

"No. You continue to wow me. I can't believe you've gotten this far without being caught."

"I am concerned that Monica and her two scientists have not returned to this island. I don't know whether they drowned in the sea or were captured by the authorities. Even if Monica is grilled for our whereabouts, she doesn't know the location of this island. The islands are far enough apart that even if they were to deploy troops to search every South Pacific island, it would take them time to travel the ocean. So I think we're very safe. What do you think about naming Malibu as the new capital of the world? The capital should be a part of the big city, it should be cosmopolitan, and have excellent weather. I thought we would build a palace on the ocean. What do you think?"

"First, let's confirm that you can hit the target in Equatorial Guinea. If the plane can't go that far, or the heat is too much, or if the trigger button doesn't detonate, we could have a whole lot of nothing on her hands."

"Oh, ye of little faith. We're going to be wildly successful in about two and a half hours. Just you watch!"

TWENTY-EIGHT

Michelle felt like she had just fallen asleep moments ago when she heard her phone ring. In normal times she would ignore it or grumpily asked who was calling her. However, she was involved with saving the world at the moment and therefore could be woken up at any time. If she needed to go out to another island in French Polynesia, she would find a way to take an iced coffee with her.

"Michelle, our analysts have been working with the boat and plane fuel calculations, and there are seven islands that are within range. None of them are private islands, but Kelly doesn't need a private island if she has all the resources she can use with her on this island. So we just have to figure out where she is."

"I'm ready to go, Sheila. I just have to stop at a coffee shop for an iced coffee on my way out of town. Can you send me pictures and coordinates of the seven islands?"

"Just a minute."

Sheila had apparently put her on hold while she spoke to someone else in the control room. Michelle waited longer than normal and wondered if Sheila had forgotten about her, but she couldn't go anywhere as Sheila had not identified the seven islands for her yet. So, she just stayed on the line waiting.

"Oh my God! We just got word that the oil refinery in Equatorial Guinea has been blown up. The officials have quite a fire on their hands. The bomb wiped out a half-mile area around the refinery. People are dead. It's a mess. They don't know how it happened yet. We have to assume it's because of the actions of Kellye Arnold. We're going to have to let our allies know of our operation to find Ms. Arnold."

"Has the team got anything out of Monica Torres yet?"

"No. This gives me an idea of how to play Monica to see if we can get more information. What we really need to know is where Kellye is hiding out."

Michelle looked at her watch and knew she'd gotten three hours of sleep this time and that it was daylight in French Polynesia, which would make searching easier. Short of going inside every house and every building on seven islands, she had no idea how she would find Kellye Arnold. She thought of one more question to ask.

"I would've thought that there would be an increase in ordering of American-type supplies for delivery to the island she's hiding out on. Have you reached out to the shipping companies to see if anyone has noticed an uptick to one of the French Polynesian islands?"

"I'll have one of the analysts run down that question. Unfortunately, it will take us some time to break through the barriers of those companies in order for them to give us information. It will be a time suck, but we will still work on it. I'm sending you information now on the islands that we need you to check. I put them in order of population as maybe you can quickly cross some of them off the list. Good luck, and Michelle, help us save the world."

"Thanks, Sheila. I'll do my best."

It was a lot chillier in Maryland than in French Polynesia. Michelle put on some different clothes and opened the door when she heard Jason's arrival with her iced drinks from the local coffee shop. She put one on one side of the backpack and poured the other into a thermos, knowing that the ice cubes would melt quickly in the tropical heat and the insulation would slow that process.

"Is this the order of the islands you're going to visit? I sure wish I could help you out in the field."

"My special talent is really useful for this situation. I'm faster than the US military," Michelle said with a smile.

She had arranged the island pictures in the order she wanted to visit them. She then nodded at Jason, offered a fist bump, and left on her island-hopping investigation.

A moment later, she was looking at lush shrubbery all around her. She knew if she didn't make serious strides in finding Kellye Arnold in the next three hours, the world would send their planes and ships to this area to help search for their suspect. Kellye had a head start on them because of the distance in the South Pacific, but the nations of the world could play catch-up quickly when all of their oil was at stake.

This first island was supposed to be uninhabited, and she moved around the major parts of the island and found no signs of life. While their suspect could be hiding somewhere in the bushes, she would still need a house and food to live and survive on, and Michelle saw no evidence of that in the first two islands she visited. Next, she had the first of a series of islands with native populations between six and eight hundred. That made it a little harder to search. The present island that she was visiting had a few beaches but mostly steep cliffs. She wondered how much the inhabitants noticed a new building or new person on another part of the island away from the population center. It was worth asking about strangers, and there were a few businesses that sold food for people sailing in the area. Fortunately, the shop-keepers spoke a little English.

"This seems like a beautiful island to live on," Michelle said to the shopkeeper.

"Yes, but it can be difficult here."

"What do you mean by difficult?"

"There are not many jobs. Everything is very expensive because it has to be imported to this island. The island is filled with slopes everywhere, and so we do not have our own airport. Imagine not having enough flat land for a runway?"

"Yes, I imagine that makes it hard to get supplies in a hurry."

"Yes, if the school or clinic needs something fast, we pay the extra cost of a floatplane to bring it here from the nearest island."

"Where do your children go to school?"

"We have a single teacher who teaches all grades and all subjects."

"That sounds like a difficult job. Do you ever have new people move here? Thanks to the internet, people can live in a tiny corner of the world and still stay connected. Do you have people like that here? They aren't natives, but they love the beauty of your island. But, of course, this island is so big that you would have a hard time knowing if anyone moved in."

"Actually, we do know if someone has moved in. The approval would go through the local government for such a sale if the person wasn't born on the island."

"Oh, that's good that you can control how much tourism your country will have."

"Yes, if you ask a shopkeeper like me on any island, we can tell you if there's a property for sale and if someone is building on it. Do you want property here?"

"It's stunningly beautiful, but we're pouring all of our money into our sailboat."

"Yeah, our last building finished a year ago. We're sorry not to have the extra laborers here to sell products to."

"I can imagine that really helps. Did someone build a new house or a new hotel?"

"The house was so big you might have thought it was a hotel, but no. These American billionaires have big homes, no? You see that in your magazines."

Michelle smiled at the shopkeeper's expression. She was trying not to be dismayed by the extravagance and yet did not want to offend a potential sale, but clearly, she didn't understand the extravagant lifestyle.

"I know what you mean. My family can live on a small sailboat, yet someone else needs a huge amount of space for very few people who rarely visit. What does the house look like? Can you see it from the beach below?"

"Oh no. It's on the other side of the island, so we don't have to look at it. The owner cut a small path up the cliff to the building. They are so rich, they keep their own floatplane. They had to buy a special fuel tank to make sure it never leaked to fuel the plane. We discussed it at the commune meeting, and the owner agreed to use it for the entire island if our generator breaks down. It's nice that we have a backup, no?"

"Has your generator ever stopped working?"

"No. But the dockworkers on Tahiti go on strike. Then, we outlying islands do not get our diesel fuel delivery. So the generator doesn't break, but we run out of fuel."

"Has the owner helped with that?"

"No. There are no lines that connect their gas tank to our generator. We keep talking about asking the owner to install pipes, but we forget about the problem when we have electricity," the shopkeeper gave a fatalistic shrug.

Michelle felt like she was going to explode with the warning bells going off in her head. She'd wanted to immediately call

Sheila, but at the same time, talking to the woman was very revealing. The least she could do was spend money in her store.

"Do you accept American dollars for payment?"

"No, but do you have a credit card? We accept that as a form of payment."

"Yes," she said, looking around the store for what she could reasonably buy.

With her credit card twenty-thousand French Polynesian Francs lighter, she left the store and looked for a place to disappear to. Other people approached the store, so she waved at them and began the walk down the path to the cove. She stopped to photograph and when no one was looking, popped into the bushes and then headed uphill toward the center of the island. She pulled her cell phone out but had no service. She then checked the satellite phone, but the tree cover was dense and getting denser. Finally, she pulled out a picture of the island and looked at a beach on the island's windward side where there likely wouldn't be any sailboats at anchor. She teleported to that beach and checked her surroundings. As soon as she determined she was alone, she checked her two phones and soon called Sheila.

"Have you found her?"

"Maybe," and Michelle proceeded to relay the shopkeeper's observations. "It's going to take me a while to figure out how to get over to that part of the island. The cliffs are steep, and between here and the other side is dense forest and uneven mountainous slopes. I want to explore the property from the woods near it, not the beach, where I bet there are cameras. I think being stealthy is important."

"How long do you think it will take you to reach this house? We don't have a lot of time. I can have resources on the island in three or four hours. She's given the world demands that we have forty-eight hours to meet. If we don't meet them, she says she'll take out a bigger target. Experts estimated that the fire will burn in Equatorial Guinea for at least a couple of weeks. We can't have her taking out any other targets."

"I've not tried to navigate this island before, and I think there are some wild horses here. If I can follow their tracks where they've knocked down parts of the forest, it will go much faster. Is there a device that can detect nearby satellite signals?"

"The agency sat phones are scrambled, so she shouldn't be able to detect your nearby position. I want another update in no more than thirty minutes. Understand that the United States Navy is repositioning ships to head toward your island. If we've made a mistake with this landowner, it will potentially slow the response to another island."

"I understand. I'll move as fast as I can. I'll call you in thirty minutes or less," Michelle thought of more questions to ask, but she heard the urgency in Sheila's voice. Most of the world was searching for this woman, and now that she's earned the label "terrorist," they needed to find her soon.

She knew she could move faster if she didn't worry about being seen by others. As this island was sparsely populated, no one would believe their eyes if they saw her appear and disappear. Better still, she didn't have to worry about random cameras catching her on film. Maybe she could learn to like deserted islands, or nearly deserted as was the case with this island, if she knew that her secret ability was safe.

In a quicker time than she expected, she was at the top of one of the mountains. The trouble was she couldn't see the coast from the view at the top. The island was like a thirty-finger hand with little coves and beaches, and she was going to have to get on the coast to find this hidden house. She knew where the main city was below and so she aimed just north of that area in the opposite direction as her starting point. She felt like she was on a giant trampoline bouncing from finger to finger except she didn't have the height. She thought she was about halfway around the island when she spotted a house just above a cove in the dip between the fingers of land. She halted and took a picture to send to Sheila. It would take a long minute to transmit via satellite, but it was worth the effort. Then she called her.

"I'm going to move in and explore that house. I'll call you if I have anything to report within fifteen minutes. If I don't call, send in the troops."

"Good luck, Michelle. I hope this is it. The oil countries have scrambled their air forces to guard their oil resources. The world is very tense at the moment, and they're mad at the United States as she seems to be one of our home-grown lunatics."

"Boss, you'll want to come here once this is over. I don't think there is anywhere like it on earth that might lower your stress than these islands. Okay, set your watch for fifteen."

They ended the call, and Michelle teleported to just inside the forest at the back of the house. She set her backpack down and dug out her binoculars. It was a nice house, and there was a marina with a dock and what looked like a boathouse. Maybe she should head there first and verify the plane. She judged where she might not be seen from the house and teleported to the edge of the structure. The danger of just teleporting inside a structure was falling or whacking herself with something already inside the structure. In this case, she chose to teleport to just inside the wall where she was standing and in the corner.

She heaved a sigh of relief not to have crashed into stuff and for there to be a floatplane. She took a picture of it, and a plate on the fuselage, and was back inside the trees a moment later. She verified that the fuselage plate and the tail number matched before transmitting a single picture to Sheila. They could run down the ownership of the plane and see if that turned up anything interesting.

She was back to using her binoculars to see what was going

on in the house. One room seemed to be a nursery. She looked around for any of the three women who had disembarked the plane in Kiribati. She looked at her watch, and it was approaching mid-day, so someone should be making lunch inside the house soon.

She also noticed she had ten minutes before her next call to Sheila. She decided it was time to take a step closer and start looking in the windows. The house was a single-story built in the island-style she had seen in her French Polynesian islands' quick tour. There were solar panels, a generator, an all-terrain vehicle, and a fuel pump. Michelle wondered if the ATV, floatplane, and generator all used the same grade of fuel. That was more than she knew about trains, planes, and automobiles, she thought with a smile. Just before she planned to look in the windows, she used the binoculars to look for cameras. After three sweeps, she didn't see any. Either the homeowner knew there was a low crime rate in this area, or they were arrogant in their assumption that unwanted guests only approached from the water.

Michelle fetched a snake camera out of her backpack and hooked it to the cellphone. She would be able to see inside the windows without her entire head showing. The snake camera was used by plumbers to look for leaks and cracks in pipes, but it worked just fine for her purpose. The first window she peered into was a guest bedroom, and it was empty. The next window was a bathroom which also was empty. The floor plan made sense as the gorgeous beach views were reserved for the kitchen, living room, and master bedroom. Before edging around the side of the building, she used the binoculars for one more look for cameras. She saw none. She looked at her watch; she had five minutes before her next check-in. If the house was empty, she would be deeply embarrassed to have the US military descend on the island by mistake. Again, she crept under a window and used the snake camera to look in the room. She spotted the woman she knew as the nanny at a table contending with a toddler. She watched for a few minutes then teleported back to the woods. She dialed Sheila.

"What did you find?"

"I used a snake camera to look in the windows. So far, I've found the nanny and David Niemi's baby daughter. I haven't found Kellye Arnold yet. I wanted to give you that update before I continued to look for our suspect. However, I think mom has to be in the area with the plane in storage and the toddler nearby. I'm going to continue searching for Kellye. When is my backup due to arrive?"

"Okay, great work! I dispatched them after your last call. I've got a couple of SEAL teams in helicopters on the way. We also have ships sailing in your direction, but they don't move that fast. They should be at your island in just under an hour."

"I'm going to see if I can find Kellye's location, and then I'll take a seat in the woods and wait for back-up to arrive. Have you figured out how she blew up the refinery in Equatorial Guinea? I don't want to charge her and cause her to blow up more oil fields."

"That's a good strategy, Michelle. We've been studying satellite film, and we believe she sent in an unmanned plane. They can travel thousands of miles, but she couldn't have launched them from the island you're standing on. So we're going back to look at records and see if David Niemi had a large purchase of them. At least then we'll know how many targets there are worldwide."

"What does she want? Is she trying to fix climate change?"

"Nope. As bad as David Niemi was, she's far worse. She wants the major countries of the world to acknowledge her as Empress of the World. She wants to be in charge of the world."

"Oh my. Why would anyone want that responsibility?"

"Exactly my thought. I wonder if Kellye ran into problems in her relationship with Niemi. She's had his child, and they've been together for three years, yet there's no sign of marriage. You know she had to have worked with Monica Torres to have him killed. I don't want you to mess with her by yourself. I'm going to have the team land and cut through the forest to you. You can share a floorplan of the house and who everyone inside is. Most of all, we must keep her fingers off any buttons. Also, we don't know the role of the sister. Is she as nutty, or is she trying to exert a positive influence on Kellye? I've got to go. Keep me posted."

TWENTY-NINE

Michelle needed to do a little more surveillance. She found the two sisters chatting in a family room at the front of the house. The windows were closed, and by its sound, an air conditioner compressor was in use. She was tempted to go inside the house to see what else she could figure out, but she didn't want to do anything that might cause the woman to set off her bombs across the world. If Kellye was using unmanned planes, at least they would take some time to reach their destinations, but knowing that they had nuclear warheads aboard meant that they couldn't be blown out of the sky without considering nearby populations.

Things looked safe at the moment, and she just wanted them to stay that way for the next hour or so. She drew a floorplan of the house, where everyone was now, and sent the diagram back to Langley. Maybe it would help the incoming teams plan a strategy. She could teleport next to Kellye's side and remove any smartphone or console from her hands. Then Sheila's special operatives' team could come in behind her and subdue the nanny and sister. Of course, if that was their game plan, she would have to demonstrate her abilities to the team, which would be a problem. She looked at her watch and saw that the team should have landed on the island by now and should be traversing toward her position.

She stood up when she saw movement outside the house. She called Sheila.

"Kellye Arnold has left the house and walked into the boathouse. I could teleport on board after she backs out, but I don't know how to fly a plane, so I'll have to take her before she gathers any speed."

"What weapons do you have with you?"

"Knife, pepper spray, zip ties."

"Okay, I want you to board that plane and spray her with pepper spray and pull her hands and feet away from any equipment. If she has a cell phone close by, throw it in your pocket or in the back of the plane, not into the water. I'll get an expert here by the time you call back on what to do with the plane."

"Thanks, Sheila."

She ended the call and watched Kellye, calculating the best moment to teleport on board. She also kept an eye out for the other two adults and the child. It would quickly become more complicated if they joined her. She jumped out of her skin when someone touched her arm. Oh my gosh, were there snakes on this island? Had she let out an audible sound?

She looked behind her and into the eyes of someone in military fatigues and a sweaty blackened face. She let out the breath she had been holding as she realized her backup had arrived.

"The suspect is in the boathouse. So far, the other three humans are inside the house. I'm going to jump aboard that plane if she backs it out of the boathouse," she whispered.

"Ma'am, we've been ordered by Langley to follow your directions." The man just shook his head in disgust and disbelief. What did she know about special operations? But that order had been repeated several times, and he had to verbally agree to it on the helo ride over to this island.

As she watched, the plane began backing out of the boathouse.

"Crap, I'm going after her. Unfortunately, I don't know anything about plane instruments, so you may need to swim out to the plane and rescue us. But know this, I will have her in custody in under a minute," Michelle said fiercely, thinking, *Empress of the World, I'm coming for you.*

Michelle teleported into the plane just as Kellye Arnold opened the door to get out of the plane. She was back in the bushes next to the special ops team before they even got used to her disappearance.

She whispered, "See, I can run fast. I wonder what she's doing. Is she loading the plane with stuff or people?"

The special ops team wasn't sure what they saw. Some were blinking. So, Michelle added, "The heat must be getting in the way of your vision." It was good to sow doubt in what they saw.

They watched Kellye perform an inspection of the plane as any pilot would. Then she exited the dock area and returned to the house. She was carrying a smartphone in her hand. Michelle looked around for a satellite dish and got an idea.

"How about if we disconnect the satellite dish? That will stop her relay of any commands, right?"

"Yes, Ma'am, but if she has a satellite phone, we only slow her down for likely a minute."

Okay, it wasn't worth doing that. As Michelle watched, the other women came out of the house with the nanny carrying the child. She had the ubiquitous diaper bag on the one shoulder. She knew that Sheila didn't want her devices going into the water, but that was her only hope to stop the future Empress of the World. She didn't want to wrestle with three women in a moving plane. When this was all over, she would take flight training so she would know what to do if she ever had to land a plane.

"I'm going to the dock, and I'm going to push our suspect and her sister into the water. The water is shallow. Then I'm jumping on the suspect to try and drown her. Can your men make a run for the dock and back me up? I'll move faster than you all will," she whispered.

"Yes, Ma'am."

Michelle pulled goggles on and checked that the pepper spray was in her pocket. Soon, she was standing in front of the two sisters and had them sprayed and shoved into the water before they got a word out. She dove off the dock and onto the suspect, wrestling her for the phone in her hand. She heard a gunshot ring out behind her and then a second shot and then boots on the dock. She felt a splash into the water next to her. She saw a male hand enter her line of vision and take control of their suspect's hand holding the phone, then another splash, and another team member had the pepper-spray-blinded suspect under control. Sheila worried about the sister and the nanny and toddler. She heard a child's wail and knew that the child hadn't been killed by the gunshot. She assumed the nanny fired the gun, which could have been dangerous if she held the toddler.

"That was awesome, Ma'am, and my men never saw a thing. You're correct that you run faster than the rest of us."

Michelle was sticking to that explanation as they moved their suspect out of the water and onto dry land. She looked around for the sister and saw her likewise escorted onto land. The difference between them was the number of swear words coming out of the suspect's mouth. The sister hadn't uttered a word. The nanny was also surrounded and had a blood-soaked shoulder from perhaps the second gunshot sound, while another special ops team member was trying to amuse the child with stuff from his equipment belt.

Michelle smiled at the team leader and said, "Hopefully, this means we just saved the world."

"I don't know yet. One of the team members deployed with us is a computer hacker. They're moving slower than the rest of us and should be here momentarily so we can see what's on that phone. The USS Francis Lightfoot has an ETA of three hours, and the French military will likely arrive soon after that. It will be an international fiasco. We've been asked to move you and our suspects off the island as soon as our nerd looks at the equipment here."

"Sounds like a good plan. It looks like your helicopter could land in this open space, or I suppose if any of you know how to fly that floatplane, we could leave on it and find your ship out in the Pacific."

The team leader smiled at her, "I was told to follow your instructions. That floatplane idea was a suggestion, so I'm going to ignore it. My helicopters are resting on one of the mountain tops of this island and will be at our service when we need them."

Michelle looked up the hillside to the woods, and a special ops guy escorted a woman out of the woods. The girl looked about sixteen and was red in the face from the heat.

"Is that your hacker? It looks like you stole her from her high school class."

"Meaning no offense on your age since you have just likely saved the world with your fast moves, the youngins can run circles around us with regard to computers. Their lack of fitness slows us down in the field, but she's an important member of my team. She can fix anything computer or mechanical. She just can't run through a rain forest, let alone run through one wearing body armor. Let me introduce you."

"Can I take off this body armor now? I don't see anyone holding guns up."

Michelle smiled at the question and replied, "Hi, I'm CIA

Case Officer Michelle Watson. Don't ever go to work for the police force. You'll be in body armor all day, every day."

"I'm Specialist Madison Hank, and I don't want to work for the police force," she said, removing her chest armor. "Where are the phones and computers?"

The Ops leader gave her the phone he had pried out of Kellye Arnold's hands when they were in the water.

"Do you know what we're looking for?" Michelle asked.

"Yeah, a program that sets off bombs."

"Maybe. We think the bombing in Equatorial Guinea was by an unmanned plane. Can you find a program that operates planes on that phone? I'm going inside the house to see what else there is."

The specialist was engrossed with breaking into the phone. Michelle made to enter the house but was yanked back before she could enter.

"Let us clear the house of any traps before you go inside."

She nodded and thought about the last thirty minutes. The three women were leaving, and one of them planned to be Empress of the World. Would she rule her empire from this house on this island? Not likely. She'd bet the house was rigged, and so she took a step back-way, way back. She remembered the luggage she'd seen when they transferred planes in Kiribati. Where did that stuff go? She decided to check the plane as it was likely not rigged to blow up as their suspect was about to fly it somewhere. She explained her thoughts to the team member who had grabbed her arm, and he had everyone back up, agreeing to search the plane first.

Sheila called as they moved toward the dock.

"Hello, we have Kellye Arnold in custody, and we're going through her stuff now."

Behind her, she heard a huge kaboom, and pieces of the house went flying. Michelle looked over at the house and then at

Kellye, who was in the water and either trying to swim with her hands tied or trying to drown herself. She couldn't tell. Finally, her splashing got the attention of one of the men, who dragged her back to shore and zip-tied her a tree.

"Michelle? Michelle?"

Michelle finally recognized that Sheila was calling her name. Unfortunately, she'd forgotten her between the explosion and Kellye's antics.

"Sorry, boss, I'm here. Our suspect apparently had a timer on her house to blow up, and it just did. Then she thought she would take the opportunity to escape, which didn't work."

"Don't scare me like that. I've been calling your name for what feels like an hour, but it was only a minute."

"I promise the next time a bomb blows up next to me that I'll call you immediately so you know I'm alive."

"I think you're getting a little punchy from the adrenaline rush and lack of sleep. I'm glad you're okay. Now, we're in the midst of a diplomatic crisis, and France is on its way to arrest our suspect. I want you to fly out as soon as possible with our boys back to the USS Francis Lightfoot."

"We're ready to go. I just want to take five minutes to search the plane. Remember, she came in loaded with boxes. Either Kellye just blew all that stuff up, or some of it is in the airplane. It's worth our while to look, but I hear you. How about if we send the first helo with our three suspects back to the ship, and then we won't be far behind. That should stop the French from intercepting our suspect. They can detain me. I'll eventually make it back home."

"Sounds like a plan. Let's do it."

Michelle ended the call and said to the special ops commander, "My boss wants us on a helo as soon as possible. Can you call the first copter and get our suspect and her accomplices out of here now?"

"Yes Ma'am."

She was impressed when she heard the noise two minutes later and then watched as a military copter landed on the beach. They quickly loaded the suspects and were off in under sixty seconds. The child was crying, but her mother should have made arrangements for the child if she didn't want her caught up in her crime spree. Eventually, the girl might end up with her father's parents, but it wasn't Michelle's concern. The second copter landed on the beach as soon as the first took off. Once the noise and wind died down from the copter blades, Michelle and one of the special ops personnel searched the airplane. They found boxes of baby supplies and a few computers. She must have loaded the plane before Michelle arrived. With the help of Madison, they decided to take all the technology and baby supplies and leave everything else behind. The warship that they were going to was not suited for an infant. The supplies of diapers would come in handy until the child could be off-loaded. Soon the second copter took off with the remaining staff involved in the operation. Michelle was dying to just teleport home, but she graciously accepted the ride to the naval ship with her own safety in mind. She took one last look at the island home that Kellye Arnold occupied, and Michelle was left wondering where Kellye was planning to go. Perhaps she was heading to the earlier island that Michelle visited and was owned by David Niemi. She sent a text to Sheila asking her to find the answer to that question. It was a small detail, but Michelle hated loose ends.

She was assigned a cabin in which she gratefully slept uninterrupted. Between the lack of sleep over the past several days, the bout of hypothermia, the adrenaline rush of the past twenty-four hours, and the fact she'd already seen her fiftieth birthday, she was exhausted. She woke eight hours later to news in an email from Jason.

Monica Torres had given testimony about Kellye Arnold and

David Niemi. The CIA was able to locate and collect all the unmanned planes ready to blow up sites around the world. Madison Hank hacked into the program and disarmed any remote control of the planes.

David Niemi was quietly buried while his daughter was adopted into his family. Kellye Arnold was judged not to be competent for trial. Her sister was charged as an accessory to the entire scheme. Sure, she hadn't encouraged her sister at any time to blow up the world's oil reserves, but she hadn't called the authorities to intervene with her sister. The nanny was given a prison sentence for firing at a federal agent and as an accessory to Kellye. The judicial system would decide what to do with Monica. She was too smart and dangerous to be on the loose. She had murdered David Niemi, but she cooperated with authorities.

Oh well, that wasn't Michelle's concern. She'd played a role in arresting a horrible human being, and now she was ready for a new case. Before the start of this case, she'd wanted a vacation in a warm climate. Now after visiting so many tropical islands in the past month, she was over that request. Perhaps she would just spend time in her California home while she waited to be assigned the next opportunity to save a fellow American or the world.

First, she had to get off this naval ship. She dressed and went to see someone as to when the ship would pull into the harbor in Honolulu. She was also hungry. She had some protein bars in her backpack, but she felt like she'd been living off them for weeks. If the kitchen area was closed because it was nearly midnight, she would ask permission to cook. She was stuck and unable to leave the ship in her normal manner of teleportation.

She was surprised to find that a French intelligence officer was waiting to talk to her, but the Navy had insisted on letting her sleep. She was a hero and deserved a quiet sleep. She was informed that the ship manned the galley around the clock, and for safety reasons, she wouldn't be allowed to cook for herself.

"I just had eight wonderful hours of sleep. I'm starving and hoping for a cheeseburger. Maybe I can help. You can send the French representative to me in the kitchen. Hopefully, he won't be put off by my eating a cheeseburger and fries."

The Naval Officer showed her to the mess deck and introduced her to the cook who invited her to take a seat while a meal was prepared for her. She was catching up on email when the French Intelligence Officer arrived. Sheila had warned her not to say much as this interview was solely to make peace with the French. Fortunately, their language barrier helped Michelle. She could pretend she didn't understand his accented questions when she didn't want to give him a direct answer. An hour later, he walked away with little new information, which was what the French should have expected when interviewing a CIA operative.

Eventually, the ship made it to Honolulu early the next morning. Michelle took the first opportunity she had to teleport back to Virginia and her home. She sighed at the peace and quiet and shivered a little at the spring temperatures in Virginia after the past few days spent in the topics.

Her doorbell rang, and she was surprised to see Jason through the peephole. She welcomed him inside.

"Hey, how's it going? You'll have to catch me up on what was happening on this end of the operation. Any long-term effects from our kayak ride across the bay in Maine?"

"Nope. I'm right as rain. Congratulations on stopping Armageddon. You're an even bigger legend with the analysts. You got bonus points for recruiting Madison Hank to our side."

"Yeah, I felt bad for stealing her from the guys who backed me up, but she was good--someone I want backing me up in the future. Since I was stuck on the ship as it traveled to Honolulu, I made a pitch to her to join the CIA. So where are you off to next?"

"Actually, it's 'we.' So the real question is: where are we off to next?"

"Oh no. Do I have time to do my laundry? Where are we heading out to? What's the case?"

"I guess Sheila wants to keep you in warm weather, so we're heading to Venezuela."

"Yikes, that country isn't on my bucket list."

"Yes, well, apparently Iran is delivering arms to Venezuela, which is governed by crazy dictator Nicolas Maduro. So, I'm heading to the airport in an hour while you get to rest and relax and join me in Panama late tomorrow. We're going to rent a boat and sail from Panama to Venezuela. So you'll have that warm weather vacation you wanted."

"Yeah, I might be changing that itinerary. I get seasick, so I might have to leave the boat except when you're leaving and coming into port. Although I didn't get sick on the Navy vessel, but it was huge and you're talking about a sailboat. Maybe I'll get a hotel in Panama or Guyana, so I can stay in the same time zone and weather as your boat. Are you a strong enough sailor to handle this? That's a long way by boat."

"I'm good. We both speak Spanish, which will help. Sheila thinks we'll get much farther into the country and might be able to stop an arms sale. By the way, Panama is in the same time zone as here, and Venezuela is an hour ahead."

"I don't know about this case," she said doubtfully. "Do you have a briefing document for me? This sounds like another really vague assignment."

He passed over a folder, "Here you go. I like your idea about Guyana. Maybe I'll book there. I'll call you from a hotel suite in whatever country I decide. So be prepared to go sometime tomorrow after four in the afternoon."

"I guess this is my punishment for being so helpful on the last case."

"Sheila said she likes how you think. You're really good at anticipating criminal decision making."

"Yeah, there's a skill to put on my resume," Michelle said with a laugh. "See you in Guyana."

THE END

ABOUT THE AUTHOR

I reside in Northern California with my rescue dog and cat. I love to travel, play sports, read, and drink wine and beer. I enjoy the diversity of the world and I'm always watching people and events for story ideas. All of my stories are generated by my imagination, I don't use AI to write books.

If you would like to sign up for my bi-weekly blog and announcement of new books, please follow this link: https://www.AlecPecheBooks.com

While you're waiting for the next story, if you would be so kind as to leave a review for this book, that would be great. I appreciate all the feedback and support. Reviews buoy my spirits and stoke the fires of creativity.

Readers that sign up for my blog receive a free prequel novelette for the Jill Quint Series.

ALSO BY ALEC PECHE

<u>Jill Quint, MD Forensic Pathologist Series</u>

Time's Up (prequel short story)

Vials

Chocolate Diamonds

A Breck Death

Death On A Green

A Taxing Death

Murder At The Podium

Castle Killing

Crescent City Murder

Sicilian Murder

Opus Murder

Forensic Murder

Return to the Scene of the Crime (short story)

Embers of Murder

Ashes to Murder

Mint Death

<u>Damian Green Series</u>

Red Rock Island

Willow Glen Heist

The Girl From Diana Park

Evergreen Valley Murder

Long Delayed Justice

Michelle Watson Series

Now You Don't See Me

Where Did She Go?

How Did She Get There?

Dog Humor

Eat, Play, Poop: Letters to my parents from camp

New Urban Fantasy Series - Stephanie Jones

The Awakening at Lake Tahoe (short story)

Witch's Medicine (2024)